STEEL

The lorry picked up speed heading down the street. It ground through the gears, the engine note rising higher and higher, growling like a beast in a cage hurling itself at the iron bars.

At precisely the right moment the lorry swerved hard, jolted over the pavement, headed straight at the kidnap house.

The steel battering ram crushed stunningly through the window. Glass and sashes sprayed, the curtain flapped wildly.

Bodie was catapulted forward. He sailed through the ruins of the window.

The noise contined to boom and baroom around in his skull; but he hit the floor on his feet, like a cat . . .

Also by Ken Blake in Sphere Books:

THE PROFESSIONALS 1: WHERE THE JUNGLE ENDS
THE PROFESSIONALS 2: LONG SHOT
THE PROFESSIONALS 3: STAKE OUT

THE PROFESSIONALS:
Hunter Hunted

KEN BLAKE

Based on the original screenplays by
Brian Clemens, Anthony Reed and
Gerry O'Hara

SPHERE BOOKS LIMITED
30/32 Gray's Inn Road, London WC1X 8JL

First published by Sphere Books Ltd 1978

Reprinted 1978

TRADE
MARK

Set in Intertype Baskerville

Printed in Great Britain by
Hunt Barnard Printing Ltd,
Aylesbury, Bucks.

Chapter One

The evening was made for music, for laughter and love – and for violence.

The Thames slid along, rippling under Waterloo Bridge, and danced with flashing, silver reflections; but as the pleasant evening progressed and the sun lowered to the horizon where London's towers chopped angular edges against the sky, crimson light flicked along the water flecking it with flakes of blood.

The popular concert at the Festival Hall had attracted a sizeable audience. The sense of expectancy filled the warm air and the scents from masses of blooms banked in their tubs soothed the lingering smell of the mud where the water lapped. People strolled along the promenade overlooking the river and lovers walked dreamily, hand in hand or with their arms about each other's waists. The long shadows in the streaming evening light, the sense of coming music, the splash from the water, all these things meant nothing to the chunky, square-built man with the cruel mouth who leaned casually against the railings of the walk.

He wore a flat cap and a hacking jacket, and by the way he stood it was clear he was tough and athletic; but he attracted no attention among the people arriving for the concert or those who walked in pairs too closely entangled with themselves to notice anything else. His hard gaze took in the cars arriving, the activity as people made their way into the Festival Hall, and noted everything with the flat concentration of a man accustomed to waiting, ready for instant action.

Laughter bubbled on the mild air. It had been a hot day and there was still just about enough light for tennis. Skateboarders, dodging the commissionaires, skimmed like miniature hang-gliders, or zig-zagged like wing three-quarters among the people on the walks. They drew annoyed looks, and sometimes smiles at the waywardness of youth; but it was a beautiful evening and life had to be lived. The evening was too golden and precious for much ill humour.

By the entrance foyer the second man who, like the first, just stood observing everything that went on, was just as powerfully built, his shoulders straining the Burberry. His hat was pulled down over his forehead; but even that anachronism attracted no attention.

A long, glistening, black official-looking limousine pulled silently into the forecourt approaching the entrance of the foyer. Its diplomatic plates gleamed in the evening light. Immediately following the limousine came a plain, four-seater saloon car.

The first observer straightened up.

Moving with an ease that disturbed no one he took off his flat cap and skimmed it over the rail. It sailed out and over and glided softly into the mud below.

The man by the entrance foyer whipped off his hat and discarded it, its function finished. He pulled down the stocking mask the hat had concealed. At once his features became squashed and appeared bloated, menacing, frightening. The lightweight Burberry flapped open as he ran out into the forecourt. The machine pistol the man produced from under the Burberry added the final note of impending horror.

Both men ran fiercely towards the long official limousine. Their machine pistols were cocked and ready.

The plainclothes security men in the follow-up car were just alighting. Another day, another assignment; but this one held an edge. The distinguished man in the limousine was Asher Biebermann, an important Israeli Cabinet Minister, and all security men the world over tautened up when Israelis were exposed in this way. But this was

London: a warm, pleasant, summer evening, and the Festival Hall with its lights and promise of music held no menace in an ordered scheme of living.

The machine pistols cracked long rippling bursts of savagery into the scene.

Two plainclothesmen went down instantly, yelling, spilling blood over the stone flags, their guns still in their holsters.

The two kidnappers, their stocking masks lending that eerie menace to everything they did, reached the limousine.

The front passenger door opened with a smash and the plainclothes security man leaped out to be met by a hail of fire that cut his legs from under him. He went down, screaming, and the two kidnappers split up. There was no need for shouted instructions. Each one knew exactly what he had to do.

Shocked cries ripped up from the crowds. People ran this way and that, the roar of the machine pistols dazing them. The front driving-side door was yanked open and a kidnapper reached in for the driver. He put up an ineffectual hand to ward off the coming blow; but the machine pistol slogged down on to his unprotected head. Chopped down with merciless ferocity he pitched headfirst out of the door and the kidnapper hauled and kicked him clear of the limousine.

In the rear the Israeli Cabinet Minister started up, shocked and horrified by the violence of the assault. His wife was flung out, sent staggering across the stone flags. The round black hole of the machine pistol's muzzle centred on Asher Biebermann.

He flinched back. He was a brave man; but the sight of the gun, hard and close and filled with death, drove him shuddering back into the upholstery. The gun jerked. Biebermann remained very still. If he was to die, he would not be the first to die for Israel.

The kidnapper up front slid behind the wheel. The engine was still running. He slapped in reverse and backed up, rapidly and jerkily, jouncing up over the pavement to reach the corner of the building and the railings.

Further along the walk a young couple, who moments before had been walking arm in arm, staggered helplessly, unable to understand what had happened. They had both been struck by stray bullets and the very violence of the shock dazed and confused them. A skateboarder, a young lad with flying hair, went on in a straight line, his skateboard hissing over the pavement.

He went straight into an iron railing and took off. The bullet that had hit him had not killed him. He toppled in a sprawl of arms and legs across the stone flags.

Wounded bystanders meant nothing to the two thugs. The limousine jerked and bounced over the pavement towards the railings. Everything was going as planned. The evening air smoked with the gunfumes and the sun slanted in long lines of orange light, and the river glittered like molten gold streaked with splashes of blood.

Across the river from the direction of the Embankment a hovercraft skittered over the water. She was a Nimbus craft, agile, fast, and she quartered across the river with a wide creamy wash spraying out on either side. She came on towards the waiting kidnappers with a buzzing noise like a bandsaw at full revs.

One of the thugs hurled a scaling net, narrow, nylon, unwrapped from his waist, out and over on to the mud. With great force he urged Biebermann over the railings. Clutching and clawing, the Israeli Cabinet Minister half-fell, half-climbed down the net. It was a six-foot drop on to the mud. The mud squelched. Greasy, gleaming, sucking, it bubbled up around the men's feet. The kidnapper urged Biebermann across the mud towards the water's edge.

Crouched at the railings, the other kidnapper sent quick bursts of machine pistol fire towards the security men in the shelter of the car. They were all wounded and two were dead and one was dying unpleasantly. Every now and then the gun sprayed a hose of death around the area, forcing people to keep back.

Siren wailing, a police car screeched into sight and slewed to a stop. Three armed policemen leaped out and ran headlong into a sleeting hail of death. They hurriedly retreated to their car, hauling one of their number who had been shot through the legs. Blood trailed after them across the road.

Free for the moment the kidnapper leaped over the railings. Ignoring the net he jumped, landing in a showering smash of squelching mud. Instantly he was on his feet, gun up, and slipping and sliding towards the others.

The Nimbus, buzzing like a giant bee, hurled for the edge of the mud and soared up, slewing around broadside on.

Biebermann was flung inboard. The first kidnapper leaped in and the second, reaching for his comrade, was hauled up.

The noise of the engine drowned out everything else and the wind bluster blattered at their senses. But as the pursuing police reached the railings of the walk and prepared to leap down a torrent of machine pistol fire met them. They were forced to drop back and retreat.

The hovercraft swung, revved up, and buzzing with a high angry whine, smashed a foaming path back across the river.

George Cowley, head of CI5, selected the red roses with care. Tonight was going to be a big night, and long-stemmed red roses, two dozen of them, fitted the bill admirably. His mood of expectancy was not quenched when he got twenty instead of twenty-four, decimalisation striking in the most unexpected places. The flower vendor smiled as Cowley paid and, holding the roses with great satisfaction, walked back across the pavement to his waiting car.

The London evening pleased him after the heat of the day. As chief of CI5 – the Squad, the Big A – he had so little time for relaxation he might never get a night to himself again for months. And CI5 had been set up by the Government to combat crime with Cowley at its head to mean business. CI5 was an élite organisation, answerable to the Government and the Minister personally. How they got results did not matter so long as those results were achieved. Cowley, who had served his time with MI5, would go all the way both to urge his men on with outrageous demands and to back them all the way against official interference. But, now, he held two dozen red roses – no, twenty red roses – and he leaned back in the front passenger seat of his Rover as Doug Waters, the driver assigned to him this night, tooled the sleek white car out into London's traffic.

The radio telephone buzzer sounded.

Cowley put the roses aside, careful not to damage them, crisp in their white paper, and picked up the receiver.

'Cowley . . . Yes . . . What ! A hovercraft . . . The Festival Hall . . . Asher Biebermann, yes – it's madness ! They won't get beyond Tower Bridge.'

He half-turned his head to shout to Waters.

'Turn around. Waterloo Bridge – fast !'

Then, back to the microphone : 'I'm on my way. Give me a situation report.'

The white Rover picked up speed, weaving in and out of the traffic, burning rubber towards Waterloo Bridge and the Festival Hall.

The site of the outrage had been speedily cordoned off and now swarmed with police. A uniformed Superintendent spoke with a mixture of respect and exasperation to Harvey, the senior police officer present, who wore plain clothes. Harvey, a big no-nonsense man with a tuft of white hair at each temple, nodded and continued speaking into his hand-held microphone.

'River police are moving down from Wapping and Limehouse. If they turn back we have another crew coming from Westminster Pier.'

Cowley said : 'And on shore ?'

'Every car within a three-mile radius. Both banks'll be crawling with men.'

Reports flowed in. Cowley's white Rover hurtled on and the news was relayed to him as it was received.

Along the river where the Nimbus hovercraft buzzed like a giant hornet, smashing the evening-gold water into a long spreading creamy-white wake, Tower Bridge hove into view. Red buses trundled sedately across and the bridge cut a fascinating outline against the darkening sky.

The kidnapper held Asher Biebermann with an expert grip, ready to quell instantly any attempt at escape. The other thug gestured quickly at the hovercraft pilot and the Nimbus swerved towards an old tumbledown warehouse. She skidded, quartering across the water and then straightened and without a pause hissed up the long slimy ramp from the river to the wharf. A derelict area showed, hemmed in by abandoned warehouses, blank-eyed with rows of boarded-up windows. The Nimbus sighed and lowered gently, coming at last to rest, the engine dying.

But another high-pitched buzzing revved up the scale.

The three kidnappers, prodding Biebermann before them, leaped from the deflated hovercraft. They ducked against the downrushing wind from the helicopter's vanes. Without wasting a second they raced for the helicopter. The door swung open, Biebermann was thrust in and the kidnappers tumbled in after.

With a roar and a gusting wind that drove rubbish away in a whirlpool of detritus, the helicopter lifted into the air.

Her vanes blurred faster and faster, glinting. She turned and swung off with that peculiar initially-airborne duck of a helicopter, buzzed swiftly off into the gathering darkness.

With the sad wail of impending distaster the last ambulance tooled smoothly away from the Festival Hall, the cordons were removed and traffic once more started to flow. The concert would go on. The people who would sit and bask in the music might enjoy themselves this evening, and perhaps hear the odd comment or two about an incident, having to wait until they switched on the news to hear what details might be released. Other men and women would have no rest until all the details were known. George Cowley looked over the scene, his wrinkled, lined, hard face expressionless. A sandy-haired man, short but tough, walking with a limp because a damned bullet still lodged in his leg, he put the fear of God into those who knew him, and was careful to limit those who knew him to a minimum.

'A helicopter,' he said, nodding. 'Not so mad at that.'

Harvey looked morose. 'Traffic Control report police helicopters on Motorways One and Four diverted to Central London.'

Cowley's instructions that all CI5 agents were to go on the Asher Biebermann snatch encompassed everyone, on leave, sick, whatever. This was the unpleasant task for which CI5 had been formed, working with any other police or security force responsible, and Cowley wanted everyone on their toes.

He looked across as the last ambulance, bell clanging, vanished, to see Bodie fishing about with a plastic bag. He pushed the plastic about so as to reveal the fired cartridge cases.

'Nine mill,' said Bodie. 'Different makes . . . Czech and East German.'

Cowley said: 'Weapons?'

Bodie wrinkled up his nose. A lean, hard, aggressive man, Bodie, who would answer to no other collection of names he might possess. Smooth, adored by the women in his life – and there were plenty of them, thankfully – he had lived the kind of life that would have fitted him for a life as a master criminal. As it was, ex-mercenary, ex-para, ex a lot of things, Bodie was with CI5 and determined that the ideals of the Squad should be upheld in this sinful world. He wore the tennis gear in which he had soundly thrashed a club champion and out of which he had fully intended to change into his new velvet suit – until the chief had called him in. Now his wrinkled nose indicated the disgust he felt.

'Sounds like they were using M.10's, Uzi's or Ingrams.'

Ray Doyle, walking up, said: 'Thought they went bust.'

'New firm in Atlanta making them now.'

Doyle held out a trilby hat. 'Snappy dressers. French – branches in Paris, Nice, Deauville . . . '

Bodie glanced at the hatband. 'Careless of them.'

'Or,' said Cowley, 'deliberate.'

Ray Doyle, round-faced, tousle-haired, but just as tough and dedicated as his partner Bodie, glanced at the tennis clothes.

'Game, set and match?'

Bodie did not smile but he flashed Doyle a sizzling glance. 'I only go for the strawberries and cream.'

Cowley ignored them. These two were his top agents, however much he might deride that idea, claiming that all CI5 men – and women, too – were the tops. But there was no getting away from it, if you wanted headlong action, iron determination, and results, then Doyle and Bodie were the men for you.

The police chief, Harvey, butted in to say: 'One of our choppers is over Kingston, starting an arc of the south west. The other one is still over the City, heading south east.'

'What about the heliport?' demanded Cowley. 'Have they put anyone up yet?'

'One in the air so far – '

'Marvellous!' Cowley held himself in check, but his shoulders hunched with the simmering rage in him. 'Caught four-square with a political hot potato.'

Bodie gestured at the Festival Hall. 'If they will go out of an evening . . . '

Doyle who knew a lot more than he let on, said with a fine touch of gallows humour: 'Apart from that, what did you think of the play, Mrs Lincoln . . . ?'

Fresh reports flowed in as helicopters on regular routes and schedules were checked out. Not a word reached the CI5 men on the get-away chopper. Cowley decided he was doing no good at the Festival Hall, scene of the crime though it might be, and so they took off for headquarters.

About the same time the shadowy shape of a helicopter made a good landing in the corner of a field. The engine was cut immediately the ship touched down. The door opened and men appeared, hustling along Asher Biebermann. He offered no resistance and appeared drugged.

Under the trees in a rutted country lane two cars had been previously parked.

The first kidnapper snapped his fingers impatiently.

'Come on, man. Keys, keys!'

The second man, Johnnie, killed the spark of anger.

'Don't panic! We're home and dry. Just don't panic.'

Frank, the first kidnapper, ignored the tone in Johnnie's voice. He swung belligerently to Mac, the helicopter pilot. Mac paused to listen as he was about to enter his car.

'You'll be at the rendezvous first. If it looks a bit off to you go to the second house. But leave your marker.'

Mac nodded and settled in the seat. 'Will do.'

With the kidnap victim in their car, Frank and Johnnie headed down the lane. The other car took the opposite direction.

A few dead leaves whirled up as the cars passed. Then quietness returned. The abandoned helicopter stood in the corner of the field, forlornly, like a dying dinosaur.

The Metropolitan Police operations centre hummed and buzzed like a sawmill. Radio messages crackled in off the air all the time. Policewomen moved flags on maps. The telephones never stopped ringing. Stalking through the midst of the bustle, Cowley prowled like a tiger, and Doyle and Bodie, flanking him, were more than a little wary of the chief.

'This is the kind of operation CI5 was set up for – set up by me! – and we've been beaten for speed. That's where they got us. This isn't a needle in a haystack. It's a whole harvest of haystacks.'

'If they haven't cleared the country,' said Bodie in his tight, helpful way. 'Transfer to a light aircraft – they're well organised.'

'Might be better for us if they have,' said Doyle.

Cowley stopped and glowered at his agents. They regarded him gravely. Cowley's face indicated clearly what he thought of their suggestions and hopes.

'And have the whole world think we can't give security to our guests! I don't believe – I simply don't believe –

they could get to the coast without someone getting a line on them.'

'A chopper's no Rolls Royce,' said Doyle. 'They make a racket – they don't just land unobserved.'

Bodie moved his hand dismissively. 'On the marshes ... a clearing in a forest ... heathland ... a golf course ...'

'Point,' said Doyle, 'taken.'

'Joe Q. Public might come through with something.' Cowley trusted he did not sound as though he was grasping at straws. 'The appeal is going out on all stations, radio and TV.'

Then what Cowley had expected occurred and there was no getting out of this one. This was one reason why he was the chief of the Big A. The summons to Whitehall was polite but peremptory, and George Cowley soon found himself closeted in a small conference room with the Minister.

The Minister was highly displeased. This hot potato was one he could well do without, and he was like to get badly burned if he didn't dump it real quick.

'This isn't Italy, or some Banana Republic. This is an island, a piece of land surrounded by water.' He leant forward to emphasis his words. 'They must not get off this island.'

'Scotland Yard, the radio and TV stations have all been swamped with calls,' Cowley told the Minister. 'It seems everyone and his mother heard or saw a helicopter in every conceivable part of London and the Home Counties.'

'And on the coast?'

'A few, but those are mostly traceable and first reports tie in with scheduled flights of civil aircraft.'

The Minister leaned back. 'What's your guess?'

'I,' said George Cowley, 'don't go in for guessing games. But I think they're down and gone to ground.'

The Minister made a small helpless gesture, revealing more than he realised as Cowley sat watching him. 'I can't tell you how serious this is. The ramifications are appalling.' Then he bore down again. 'Don't keep this one under your hat, George ... I want a fully co-ordinated operation, police, special service, whatever.'

'I understand but, in the final analysis, weight of numbers may be an embarrassment. This is clearly a well-planned operation by a small force of, as yet, unknown participants.'

'The word embarrassment is well chosen but, equally, we must be *seen* to be active. We cannot afford to risk the criticism of *appearing* inactive.'

'Those are political considerations, Minister. We have the experience of other countries to ponder on. Cities saturated with counter-terrorist forces, drenched with operatives and – weeks, months, later – the kidnappers' quarters have been uncovered – empty! Marvellously anonymous places. Not derelict farm buildings miles off the beaten track.' Cowley knew what he was talking about. 'But flats or houses in the thick of suburbia or right in the heart of city centres.'

'I know, I know . . .'

'I assure you, Minister, our best course is to play the waiting game. They will. And so will we.'

What Cowley knew and did not say was that at the end of the waiting game they might find merely a bloody corpse. But all his experience told him he was right. He was not gambling; it was sheer professionalism.

Chapter Two

The suburbs of London can be vast, anonymous sprawls of brick and concrete for those who wish to shrink away from the glare of publicity. Neighbours come and go and, sometimes, a few polite words are spoken. Unless you want to talk, and you need never do so, you can remain completely unknown.

The row of terrace houses, built sometime before the First World War, still held together defiantly against time and weather and bombs. The gap where numbers 20, 22, 24 and 26 had vanished one night in 1940 had been built up with red-brick boxes, smaller and tighter than the grimy, grey-bricked houses flanking them. Farther along, at the end of a terrace, the houses were more run-down, but they were still habitable. In some front gardens with the privet bushes a few flowers struggled to bloom.

On the night of the kidnapping of the Israeli Cabinet Minister one of these anonymous houses showed a chink of light from an upstairs bedroom. In the room the big old double bed had been dismantled. The mattress squatted on the floor in a corner. Sleeping bags were rolled beside the mattress. A bedside lamp stood on a bentwood chair.

The bulb was too powerful for the lamp and cast odd shadows in the room. They gouged deep pits of darkness beside the huddled man lumped on the mattress in the corner. His wrists and ankles were bound and he was blindfolded. He just lay there. One shoe shone with a gleam of black polish above the crusted mud from the Thames. On his other foot the sock showed rumpled and dragged down.

The kidnapper, Frank, hunched on the edge of the mattress, half-awake but still alert. He looked up when the door opened and Johnnie walked in with a tray of food; but he did not speak. Johnnie put the food tray down beside Frank and then bent to the bound and gagged man.

'Don't suppose you had time for a little pre-concert dinner,' said Johnnie in a light, almost conversational tone. He untied Asher Biebermann's hands. 'Sorry it's not salt beef and knockles or knoodles – or what is it, lotkes?'

When the gag came free Biebermann gasped a shuddery breath. His face was shrunken and looked years older than it had when he'd driven up in the big limousine with the prospect of a concert before him. The blindfold remained firmly over his eyes shutting out the light and the man who had kidnapped him.

Johnnie lifted a plate of tinned stew. He profferred a spoon.

'You must excuse the cutlery,' he said, enjoying himself. 'Don't want you cutting yourself.'

As Biebermann groped blindly for the spoon, Johnnie took his hand and held it lightly before placing the spoon between the fingers.

'Nice hands.' There was a deeper meaning in his words. 'You should play the piano with hands like that.'

On a gasp, unable to stop himself, Biebermann said: 'I do.'

'Yes,' said Johnnie, watching the hand in his grasp. 'Very musical, you people. Beethoven, Strauss – he wasn't one of your lot was he, Strauss? Tales of the Vienna Woods, that one?'

The rigmarole of nonsense washed over Biebermann. The pressure of Johnnie's fingers increased and he turned the captive's hand over, still inspecting it with the look of a wolf.

'Hope we don't have to chop one off.' He spoke quietly, easily. 'One of your fingers.'

Biebermann, after that single short breath, remained silent and waiting for what was to come.

'Reminds me,' said Johnnie. 'Reminds me of the fellow who went in the nut house – nervous breakdown – he asked the doctor if he'd be able to play the piano when he got out. The doctor said of course he would. The man said: "Funny. I couldn't before I came in . . . " You understand?' An edge of impatience broke in Johnnie's light voice. 'You up on the language?'

Biebermann nodded.

'We will, you know.' And now the menace was naked and unmasked in Johnnie's voice. 'If we have to. We'll chop your hand off, if we have to . . .'

He wrapped Biebermann's fingers around the spoon and guided his other hand to the edge of the plate.

Looking silently on, Frank sipped from a can of beer. He knew they were not playing games. But he did not laugh at Johnnie's joke. He had told it to Johnnie . . .

Although George Cowley might, in his acerbic way, refer to Doyle and Bodie as his knockabout twins, they were professionals to their finger tips. When the searches laid on by the Army in likely locales at last turned up the abandoned helicopter, Bodie and Doyle were on the scene – fast.

The car skidded the last few yards and the doors swung open. The partners leaped out and made for the helicopter where soldiers were standing guard and others were searching around.

'Don't trample all over the place!' sang out Doyle, running across.

One of the soldiers looked up with a hurt expression.

'We found it!'

Bodie was amused. 'You'd have a job to miss it. Anybody touched the outside of this thing?' At the shaking of heads, Doyle went on to give orders for a controlled search. Then he went over to join Bodie at the machine.

Bodie glanced up. 'Hang about – could be booby-trapped.'

Doyle looked through the canopy. 'You think they're that fancy?'

'They pinched a helicopter,' Bodie pointed out. 'Snatched a guy some Arabs would give a stretch of desert for. I'd say they weren't too sensitive about blowing off the odd limb or two.'

'You're a convincing talker when you're in the mood. I'll leave it for the Bomb Disposal boys.'

He backed off and then the partners began to cast around near the machine, going through the gap into the trees. Bodie called, softly, and Doyle joined him. Then, very carefully, using a twig, Doyle turned the single black shoe over.

'Kayser, Tel Aviv. Supports local industry.'

'Be hopping around on one foot,' said Bodie. 'Except he's not going to be going very far.'

They moved on, despite their facile remarks keenly alert to any and everything about them. They found the tyre marks of the kidnapper's cars.

'Looks like two cars.'

'One goes one way,' said Doyle, looking along the two sets of tracks. 'One the other. Take your pick.'

Police were arriving on the scene; but even with their help the trails soon petered out – both of them. Feeling that they'd made a start but where it had led wasn't worth too much, the partners returned to HQ. As CI5 men they were contacted at once and Harvey told them the latest news. But Cowley was tightly closeted with the Minister, and nothing, not even two top-flight CI5 operatives, could dislodge the chief until the Minister was through. They stood fuming in the lobby.

'It's incredible,' said Doyle. He pushed a hand through his curly hair, looking exasperated. ' "The Minister cannot be disturbed." If Smiler got through on the hotline it would be the same.'

'Listen,' Bodie told his partner with the wiseacre act in full spate. 'You've got to learn to live with the order of things. There's a move afoot to bring back touching the forelock.'

'Does it hurt?'

Bodie, about to attempt an answer to that, looked up and saw Cowley and the Minister descending the staircase. 'Here they come. Get your forelock ready.'

Cowley looked just as unruffled and tough as he liked to appear to his men; but: 'Sixteen hours since they did the job. They're in no hurry to get in touch. We just have to wait.'

The Minister's professional politician's cool was still in place; but the strain was beginning to get to him.

'Try telling that to world governments. Washington still believes that over here everything stops for tea.'

'What,' said Cowley in his aggressive way, 'about that little matter of D-Day?'

'Ah, but,' said the Minister. 'They were right with us.'

Then Cowley was spared any more, as, reaching the lobby he saw Doyle bustling across. His tough pugnacious face was set in lines both of triumph at Cowley's correct assessment and anger at their own apparent helplessness.

'It's happened, sir. They rang *The Express*. There's something waiting for us in a phone box –'

'Next step in the Waiting Game,' observed Cowley. He did not smile. It was still only the beginning of what might yet be a ghastly tragedy blazoned all over the world, and with the British Security Forces as the inefficient scapegoats.

The Minister frowned. 'I don't like the sound of the "something".'

It had to be Bodie who said: 'Half an ear, perhaps . . .'

Cowley hustled forward and collected Bodie on his way out. Doyle tagged along, enjoying what Cowley had to say. For the chief of CI5, in his most icy vein, told Bodie: 'There are times, Bodie, when I find your ribaldry quite distasteful.'

They took Bodie's car and made a fast drive through the London traffic, hurtling along with the foot well down. The phone box standing isolated on a corner with office buildings gloomily frowning down was unmistakable. A couple of police cars with blue lights flashing were parked up the side street and the area had been roped off. The senior police officer, Harvey, was waiting for them.

Cowley gave him no time for the formalities.

'How soon did your men get here?'

'Within seven minutes, sir.'

As Cowley nodded, only half-satisfied, Doyle pulled on rubber gloves with a snap and Bodie peered cautiously into the phone box. Traffic grumbled away in the street; but the sounds seemed oddly muted to the men absorbed in what this phone box might tell them of the kidnappers.

'Every chance the box hasn't been used since.' Cowley looked across at Bodie who turned away from his inspection.

'He'd use gloves and a pencil to dial with – '

'Possibly.' Cowley knew damn well there was no real possibly about it. But he finished: 'There's always a chance.'

Doyle eased the door open as though he was stealing the Crown Jewels. He scanned the interior of the box, very carefully and very slowly, trying to figure if anything looked – odd. The defacement was as usual, the phone grubby, the floor filthy, the phone books tattered – a plain manila envelope wedged between the books . . . a brand new, shiny envelope . . . Carefully, carefully, Doyle lifted the envelope. He brought it out of the box as though carrying a nest of vipers and placed it on the ground where a technical officer ran a metal detector over the innocent-looking manila. Doyle put his head on one side.

'There's something bulky in there – look at the outline.'

Bodie was the first to say: 'A cassette?'

With a nonchalant skill that held down a tight-lipped expectancy of immediate disaster the envelope was sussed clean and Doyle snipped it open with the scissors he took from the technical officer. He pulled out, very gingerly, a cassette and a coloured Polaroid photograph.

Bodie peered at the two objects. 'Cassette's German. Not too much "Buy British" about this lot.'

Doyle held the Polaroid print between his rubber-gloved fingers. 'Not much of a swinger, either. Bit cheapskate. They've used available light.'

They looked at the coloured print of Asher Biebermann. The print was not too good, fuzzy and criss-crossed by odd shadows and lines; but there was no mistaking the Israeli Cabinet Minister.

'He looks a bit groggy,' observed Cowley. His voice betrayed nothing of what he was feeling.

'Doped to the eyeballs,' agreed Doyle.

'Let's get it blown up. And let's get somewhere where we can hear this tape.'

That somewhere turned out to be the Met ops room rather than CI5 HQ. The police brought in an electronics wizard and a portable cassette player that could have taken in messages from the Moon. Two Israeli Embassy officials were present and the senior, Hirschfield, bore a look on his weathered and experienced face that, in its grief and resolution, owed nothing to playing a part. The voice of Biebermann sounded hoarse, breathy, and he hesitated as he spoke throwing unnatural pauses between the words of the message.

'. . . will be released unharmed, otherwise my . . . captors will consider themselves absolved from the consequences.'

Hirschfield, concentrating, leaning forward, tensed and absorbed, said: 'That last section – once more if you please.'

The engineer hit the rewind, stopped the tape, set it playing again. Biebermann's voice echoed again in the ops room.

'. . . are met in full, I will be released unharmed, otherwise my . . . captors will consider themselves absolved from the consequences.'

Hirschfield looked up. On that tense face a tiny glint of satisfaction showed. 'Thank you. He tells us two, possibly three, things.' He gestured at the cassette player. 'We had to hear it several times. The pauses. The seventh word – the eleventh – the seventeenth.'

Cowley nodded, caught up in the tenseness. 'A prepared code . . .'

Bodie said: 'In a message dictated by the kidnappers?'

'He tells us,' said Hirschfield, and he spoke to them all. 'They are not Arab, they are not Political. They are, I think, British.'

Bodie looked admiringly at the cassette and its hidden secrets. 'And if they'd been – Arabs, politicals – a different sequence.'

Hirschfield had no need to smile at Bodie. 'We have to be prepared at all times – on all levels.'

'Quite,' said Cowley, pushing his heavy glasses back. He looked up as a white-coated photo-lab technician entered with the blown-up prints of the Polaroid photograph. He began to lay them out on the table methodically, one by one, as though preparing for a game of Patience. They all saw the vividness of the image.

'My, my,' said Cowley, putting down the last blow-up. 'There's carelessness for you. Shadow of a tree. A break for us – that bit of morning sun for the picture.'

'In the worst summer for years,' said Doyle.

'They say that every year.' Bodie jerked his forefinger at one of the prints. 'Look, this line. It's not a crease – '

'Telephone line?' suggested Doyle.

'Perhaps.' Cowley studied the enigmatic line across the picture. 'But there's no proof it's on the outside. The window's here. This round patch, now. I don't think it's a stain.'

'Could just be a ventilator disc.' Bodie turned the print at a right angle, squinted at the disc. 'You see them in converted houses. Bedrooms turned into bed-sitters – gets rid of cooking smells.'

'It's very faint,' said Cowley.

Doyle said: 'Plastic – on glass – would be.'

'What about this, sir.' Bodie drew Cowley's attention at once by the way he spoke. 'The hard edge with the left-hand curve?'

'Bit of furniture,' suggested Doyle. 'Obstructing the sunlight.'

With a riffling gesture Cowley scooped up all the prints and stuffed them into the outstretched hand of the lab technician.

'Bigger! Bigger still! Especially that round blob.'

The photo-lab tech clasped the prints to his bosom and went out, already figuring angles and exposures. Cowley turned to the two Israeli Embassy officials. He was well aware how delicately he must needs tread, and he accepted that as a part of his function as chief of CI5.

'Thank you, gentlemen. We knew about the British angle. They collected the helicopter from Elstree airport on forged documents. Unusual. Professional criminals meddling in the political area. I don't like it.'

'It's happened elsewhere,' pointed out Hirschfield. 'If I or any of our specialists can be of any – '

'Specialists, Mr Hirschfield? Don't tell me you have specialists operating here . . . '

'No, Mr Cowley.' Hirschfield spoke with sauve gravity. 'I am not telling you that.'

The police canteen rattled and echoed with canteen noises, hard spurting edges of sound. Knives and forks hitting trays, the scrape of chairs, the clatter of thick cups in thick saucers. The smells were divine to a starving man and a trifle thick in the middle to a well-fed copper wanting to put his feet up. Bodie and Doyle queued where the smells were thickest, shuffling along with their trays in line. Steam hissed and the chatter filled the canteen, and Bodie, for one, was not pleased.

'I was thinking of a bit of Aylesbury duck at Simpson's in the Strand. I suppose you're used to this toad-in-the-hole stuff.'

'Don't give me that.' Doyle lifted his tray and turned to the pay desk. 'It's a wonder you don't still eat out of a billy can.'

Bodie tried to catch the girl's attention, saying: 'I think I'll try the spotted dick – if I *can* get the young lady's attention.'

Doyle looked at the tables and moved in on one with two vacant seats. The other two seats were occupied by a couple of women police officers, a couple of highly attractive police officers.

'Mind if I join you?' Doyle's round cheerful face positively beamed.

The dark-haired girl with the impish look about her said: 'We're not coming apart.'

Doyle sat down and, meaningfully, said: 'I can see that.'

The second girl, whose blonde hair sheened immaculately under the strip lighting, looked interested. 'C Division?'

'No.' Doyle lifted a fork. 'CI5.'

The dark-haired girl was impressed; but determined not to show it. 'Mmm. Big stuff. Shouldn't you be in the private dining room?' That, she felt, ought to cut him down to size.

Doyle, enjoying the tease, smiled. 'I'm not dressed for it.'

Carrying his tray with something of the air of a stable-boy carting his bucket, Bodie moved in. His smoothness was in full evidence. 'Afternoon, girls. Is this man annoying you?'

The blonde was well up to this ploy. 'We were discussing sexual politics, when your friend arrived. Is it within your brief?'

Bodie sat down. 'Brief or briefs?'

The dark-haired girl raised her eyebrows. 'They're hung up on clothes.'

'Prisoners,' observed the blonde, 'of the virility cult, obviously.'

Both Bodie and Doyle were enjoying the verbal catch-as-catch-can, it made a welcome break; but Doyle's intercom cheeped, a monstrous intrusion on the fun and games.

Doyle took out his intercom, swallowed, said: 'Yes, sir . . . ' He listened intently. 'Will do.' He stowed the radio away and started to rise. 'Come on. We're on.'

Bodie let his poised knife and fork hover over his uncut pie. He looked up and a crease dinted down between his eyebrows.

'On what?'

'On a bus! Come on.'

Doyle moved away and Bodie furiously snatched up his pie. It was hot. He had to toss it from hand to hand. He saw the two girls laughing at him. 'Perhaps we can continue this discussion at a later date.' He moved not towards the waiting Doyle but nearer the blonde. He leered on her, a beautifully respectable and yet highly-promising type leer. 'You and I could form a sub-committee and throw it open for general discussion – afterwards. Meanwhile, you're welcome to the chips.'

Feeling that he had preserved some of the charisma of CI5 and particularly of one of its brightest stars, he hurried after his partner.

The information Cowley extracted from the new blow-ups sent every man and woman available out and on to the streets of London. It was a long shot, an incredibly long shot; but Cowley felt in his bones that just as long shots had come in before, this one would, too. He'd told Harvey his thoughts on that puzzling shadow with the rounded edge to it that the prints still did not fully reveal.

'I think that shadow is *outside* the room. If it is, I reckon it could be a bus.'

Harvey pulled his nose. 'There are three hundred bus routes not counting the As and Bs and then there are the Green Line double-deckers . . .'

'There is enough daylight to give us at least one sweep.'

'Then the locations, if any fit the bill . . . There'll be dozens.'

'I know.' Cowley did, too; but his own eagerness would not be put down. 'But we *do* know several things already. The room faces East, there's a tree outside; the line – if it is a phone line – can't be less than twenty-four feet from the ground. The infra-red process suggests grid lines in the disc – it very probably is a ventilator.'

So that was why Doyle and Bodie finished up their interrupted meal on the front seats of the top deck of a red London bus.

Bodie was eating his pie and speaking in between. 'This is ridiculous.'

'Why?' demanded Doyle. 'We weren't going to get anywhere sitting around police canteens.'

'I could have put the fix on the blonde one. Sexual

Politics! This equality business is definitely not good for what the Mexicans call *cojones*.'

'Quite. Now, if that hard edge with the curve *is* the top of a bus, this is the place to be.' Doyle unfolded the route map and spread it out.

'You,' pointed out Bodie, 'were the one who said it was a chest of drawers.' He finished up his pie. 'It's daft sticking us on a bus – we should be where it's at.'

'They're pouring people on to buses, the entire Greater London area. Cops, troops, airmen, navy – two by two, like the Ark.'

Then the banter ceased as a house hove into view that bore some of the vital statistics they were looking for. They both stared hard through the window, noting down everything in their camera-minds.

'That's the third on this route.' Doyle marked the map.

'No phone line.'

'I don't think that line was outside the room. Could be a bit of string run across to dry dish cloths, nylons, anything.'

'Report it, anyway. I reckon we're about a mile from the depot. What's our next jaunt?'

Doyle started to call in on his radio, saying aside to Bodie: 'A fifty-two.'

Bodie said in his most high-flown disgusted way: 'Further out? They speak a different language!'

'Keep your eyes peeled.' Doyle had been a policeman and he was well aware his views sometimes did not altogether coincide with Bodie's. On the matter of keeping an observation, for example. The volatile Bodie would let it all hang out and be damned, whilst Doyle, just as explosive, could buckle down and keep it all in there, hard and on the job.

All over London, keen-eyed men travelled the streets, jolting along on the top decks of red London buses, looking for a house, for a special house that had all the factors revealed in the Polaroid print.

Bodie and Doyle ran the check on the fifty-two's route and were recalled to the Met operations centre. Cowley wanted them handy, and if he would never admit, even to himself, any reason for feeling comfort at the near presence of Doyle and Bodie, the fact remained. Doyle and Bodie were – good – to have around.

All the same, his hard-lined face clamped down as they came in and with that characteristic gesture he swung his heavy glasses off and dangled them, accusingly, like a pair of handcuffs. 'You took your time.'

'We were way out, sir,' said Bodie.

'Neasden, sir,' amplified Doyle. 'Gateway to the West.'

Cowley ignored the nonsense even as he admitted its existence, its valuable existence in a situation where a man might be excused for sitting down and shaking to pieces. The Israelis were fully within their rights to blow their collective tops. The job was hair-triggered-wired-to-dynamite. And it was down to him, to George Cowley. Well, that was one of the things he was paid for . . .

'They were a mite too quick for us. But that's their prerogative – for now. They put their message across and got off the line before we could trace the source – it was somewhere here.'

He tapped the map spread on the table, repeating those pinned to the walls. Doyle looked down at the fine-drawn lines of the streets, a wriggling-worm factory of tiny street after tiny street.

'Oh, great.' Doyle looked at Bodie. They knew those mean streets.

Cowley hit the play button of a portable cassette recorder.

'We have recorders placed in every newspaper office, the periodicals, radio, TV, everywhere. Now, listen.'

The voice from the speaker sounded tinny. 'Newsdesk?' When the answering voice confirmed, the speaker went on, swiftly and without a pause. 'Get this down and be quick about it. If they want Biebermann, he's up for grabs.'

'Just a minute – ' The newspaperman sounded surprised; yet both Bodie and Doyle, listening intently, caught the note of play-acting. The newspaperman understood, then . . .

'Never mind the just a minute!' The kidnapper's voice harshened. 'Get it down. He's up for grabs. The highest bidder. One lot might want him back. The other lot might want him put away. We want to make a sale. Get that?'

'You want to make a sale . . . '

'Right! The next call we make we'll state our terms. But tell 'em to get their minds made up. There'll be no hanging about.'

A harsh and final click and then the line went dead.

Cowley watched his two top agents.

Bodie screwed that handsome face up.

'I thought it was Jimmy Flynn for a bit. But he's inside for a long one.'

Doyle shook his head.

'Familiar. What we need are voice prints. Fingerprints aren't enough any more.'

Cowley pressed the stop button and the cassette recorder stopped humming.

He wondered what else wouldn't be enough any more before they tied this one up. He refused the next and obvious thought – *if they did*. They were going to. That was what CI5 was all about.

Chapter Three

The news hit like a volcano erupting. Telephones rang incessantly, conferences were held at every level; but it all boiled down to the single hateful fact. An important Israeli Cabinet Minister had been kidnapped and was being held securely. His life was up for auction. The bidders were there aplenty, so Cowley imagined. He went along to the Nadim Investment Group wondering just how much anyone – or any group – was willing to pay for a life.

Doug Waters dropped Cowley off at the discreetly sumptuous entrance with its marble and gilt, and tooled the Rover away into the parking area. Cowley went inside. The foyer was expensively furnished with free-standing statuary and all along one wall a logo involving palm trees and oil rigs. There were real drooping palm fronds in ceramic pots of Ali Baba size. The legend NADIM INVESTMENT GROUP was picked out in gold leaf against the marble in English and Arabic. The leather furniture was immense and engulfing. Everybody moving about the foyer was smartly dressed and most of them wore Arabic clothes. The whole atmosphere was discreet and orderly.

Cowley met his contact, a hawk-faced man, immaculately dressed, who was, so Cowley assumed, a highly-placed executive with diplomatic connections. The Arab gestured gracefully as he spoke.

'Of course one knows about the auction as you call it. There are Arabic newspapers printed here, too, you know.'

Cowley nodded. 'With political agents on their staffs. Would they want Biebermann?'

Speaking in an oblique way that puzzled Cowley, the Arab said: 'Dead or Alive . . .'

'I'm sorry, you're not making yourself clear.'

'Then I'm sorry, too.' The Arab paused. 'The Israelis have always refused to negotiate. Acts of War and so forth. This is somewhat different. Mr Cowley, you are not normally obtuse. Biebermann is held by criminals, not by soldiers in a State of War. No one condones criminality.'

'No. No, of course not.'

'I hope that was not intended as a cynicism.'

'No,' said Cowley, evenly, his voice nicely modulated. 'It was not.'

'If a certain group were to assist in obtaining Biebermann's freedom – that group would be undertaking the unpleasant task of trading with criminals and – for using their good offices – would surely expect considerable concessions, certain acts of amnesty.'

'That,' observed Cowley, 'sounds a little close to direct demands, direct exchanges between the two sides.'

The Arab did not smile; but his elegant hand waved downwards at Cowley. 'Perhaps we are now in the diplomatic area. Perhaps you should consult your superiors . . .'

'Yes.' Cowley had one thing sorted out, at any rate, and could file it away and get on with the job. But he remained perfectly polite. 'Yes, indeed.'

The bedroom of what Cowley and his men would call the kidnap house remained as before, with the glaring lamp slowly burning a brown stain into the shàde, and the saggy mattress spread on the floor. Asher Biebermann, bound and gagged and drugged, sprawled in his corner, a crumpled lump, unconscious of his suffering.

Johnnie slumped also, but he sagged in sleep, hunched over his gun.

Very gently the door opened. Frank looked in. A frown crossed his face and his harsh mouth tightened.

He stepped in.

'Hey, hey, hey . . .'

Instantly, Johnnie's head snapped up and his hands

curled around the machine pistol. He roused himself; but before he could speak, Frank spat out at him.

'What're you on? Uppers or Downers?'

Johnnie relaxed his grip on the machine pistol.

'I'm on nothing!' He spoke defiantly, angry that he had been discovered half-asleep, ready to argue it out. 'I don't need stimulants. Money stimulates me.' He licked his lips. Especially the lack of it.'

Frank checked the bindings on Biebermann's wrists and ankles and, satisfied they were still tight, moved to the door. He jerked his head peremptorily at Johnnie, a tight little command to follow.

Johnnie followed Frank on to the landing; but he hovered in the door, looking back at the prisoner. He was reluctant to let Biebermann out of his sight.

Frank spoke with a half-laugh, half-curse. 'Houdini wouldn't get out of that.'

They moved into the second bedroom, just as bare and barren as the first. A deal table, dusty and half-covered with newspapers, held a glittering array of sharp instruments. The scalpels and saws and knives gleamed brilliantly alongside tins of Main Course soup, cans of beer, packets of biscuits and a greasy packet of butter. Johnnie looked down. Then he picked up a surgeon's knife and held it, looking up at Frank.

'Sharp?'

'Sharp as my wife's tongue.'

'Where is she?'

'Majorca.'

Johnnie nodded, thinking of days on sunny beaches and the birds and the luxury of living high on the proceeds they would get from this little job. 'Palma?'

'No.' Frank shook his head. 'Too crowded. Along the coast.'

Johnnie slid the knife carefully along his palm, like an old-time barber.

'Well, we'll see how they respond to our next little trick . . . '

He put the knife down, carefully, ranged neatly alongside the other instruments. Frank picked up a can of beer and snapped it open with a sharp crack. Froth spurted.

Johnnie went back across the landing to the other bedroom to check on Biebermann. He was securely tied, as Frank had said; but Johnnie saw not a bound and helpless victim but the work he had put in as a means to sunshine and beaches and birds . . .

The day had been long and exhausting. Leg work they used to call it. Now they ought to call it bus work.

In the large and shinily-polished washroom with its array of basins, its chrome taps, its stalls, its mirrors, its dispensers, its highly-coloured and admonitory notices, Cowley, Bodie and Doyle made the habitual movements of putting themselves back together again as human beings.

Standing planted in front of a mirror, Bodie was shaving. Unkind people would say he admired the view. Bodie wasn't that far gone yet; but, even if he had been, he'd have been in the right of it.

Doyle, still unshaven, hunched on a bench against the wall by the waste-paper bin. Like them all, he was tired. He was listening to messages on his handset, the intercom balanced awkwardly.

Cowley was busily fighting his way through the maze of pinning and wrapping enveloping his new shirt like concentration camp guards. He pricked himself and felt too damned mean to cuss. He did complain about the shirt, however . . .

'I specifically asked for a plain poplin shirt – my colour, white, blue – '

Bodie said: 'Pink.'

'What?'

'Pink, sir. It's a very in shade just now.'

Cowley looked with distaste at the half-unwrapped shirt. 'Oh, really? What I specifically did not want were bold stripes.'

The boldness of the stripes on his new shirt would have made a prison warder sit up and take notice.

Abruptly Doyle swung his legs off the bench and sat up.

'They might have a touch!'

Cowley turned on him. 'What's that?'

'They've more or less eliminated twenty-three sites reported in on the bus routes. But seven are still under full surveillance. They turned over a bunch of junkies in one. And another is looking very special!'

Cowley flummoxed around with his jacket, sticking his arms in, flailing about. His tie was not tied. 'Where man, where?'

Doyle stood up. 'Neasden – sir.'

Bodie moaned. 'Oh, no . . .'

Reassuringly, Doyle told his partner: 'No. Not one of ours. The one Johnstone told us about. On a corner, with the lane at right angles, end of terrace?'

'Well,' stormed Cowley, hauling his jacket straight. 'Didn't you check it out?'

'We followed instructions. Stayed on the bus.'

Cowley did not explode. He was on his way, snapping back like a rear-gunner: 'Come on!'

Bodie had the shaving foam wiped off now – or most of it. He snatched up the tube, the razor, and the bottle of after-shave. Swinging his jacket – his incredibly expensive and well-cut jacket – from the other hand and trying to stuff the shaving gear into the pockets, Bodie followed the other two out. It was all go.

The locales in which action might erupt at any time should not have occasioned any surprise in the tough cases of CI5. The evening breathed about them as Cowley swirled his white Rover into the forecourt of an Asian cinema, darkened now and with just the few lights showing. The posters were mere dark rectangles, with an occasional lurid splotch of colour, a sari, a tulwar, the trunk of an elephant, springing isolated from the darkness.

The three men alighted on the run and made for the entrance steps, concrete and broken-edged, the iron railings chipped.

On the move, Cowley snapped out: 'I want no precipitate action; no heroics. This is a highly delicate matter. If anyone gets any ideas, remind them of the Cyprus debacle.'

The swing doors with their darkened red paint opened and light spilled out to reveal suddenly the handsome, dark, daredevil face of the Asian hero, posed, and the bejewelled maiden over whom he both leaned and yet retreated from.

Doyle nodded to the poster as they went in and, in a low voice, to Bodie said: 'I've seen it. The hero had an operation to get his hand off his hip.'

'Apart from that, Mrs Doyle, what did you think of the show?'

Cowley paused for a moment, almost but not quite exasperated. 'Bodie, Doyle.' His voice was brisk enough. 'A man's life is at stake.'

Together, the partners said: 'Yes, sir.'

Two men moved forward in the half-lit foyer to meet them. The local police chief looked worked up, not nervous highly charged. He bore down ready for trouble.

'Mr Cowley?'

Cowley's ID whipped out, flipped open, was as swiftly replaced. 'I am.' The police chief produced his own ID and the four men followed by the local man's plainclothes detective assistant headed for the rear exit. Cowley looked up. 'Nothing on?'

'Three times a week,' the chief told him. 'And the odd bingo session. The house under surveillance has been empty for some time, except for occasional visits by two men, both unknown to the woman next door.'

'What about the neighbours? Did you find them somewhere to stay?'

'Yes, all arranged. Divorced lady and her daughter. The girl's nine. They're down the front. Want a word?'

Along the rows of mute seats tiny under the sweep of roof two figures sat in the front stalls. The place exuded a ghostly, musty air, most odd. Footfalls fell muffled. The woman and her daughter, ordinary folk, a little bewildered by the sudden activity that had befallen them, were sipping tea from paper cups. Cowley threaded his way through the upturned seats to reach them. He felt, as always, a little helpless, when innocent people were brutally exposed to the nerve-tingling unpleasantness that was daily life to him and his men.

'Well, well, well,' said Cowley. He spoke to the girl and his craggy face wore the most amazingly gentle smile. 'This won't do, a young lady like you up at this time of night.' His smile remained, genuine and unforced, as he spoke to the girl's mother. 'Good evening, madam. I'm sorry you've been disturbed like this. You understand what's happening?'

'Good evening . . . The Chief Constable said you suspect something's going on – '

'Yes. Some bad lads, possibly. A hide-out, perhaps. You've seen some comings and goings, I understand?'

'Yes, a couple of men. Very ordinary. Working men. I thought perhaps they were going to do it up, decorate or something.'

'Very ordinary? But villains mostly are. That's what people tend to forget.' His smile remained. 'It's not like it is in the comics.' He spoke to the girl and she regarded him gravely over the rim of her paper cup, wide-eyed. 'No baddies with eye-patches or twirling moustaches. Now, we must get you away to get some sleep.' To the mother he spoke with a brisk directness he hoped might reassure her. 'Don't worry. We won't make a mess. May we have the keys?'

As the divorced woman who, Cowley shrewdly suspected, might be taking a thrill from all this, handed him the keys, he nodded again, very politely, and said: 'Thank you. Good night.'

Back through the tipped-up seats Cowley reached the local chief. He held the keys in his hand. 'What are you going to do with them?'

'Small hotel,' said the chief. 'Bed and breakfast.'

'Nice place?' Cowley felt for the woman and her child. 'Clean and comfortable?'

'Yes. Of course.'

'Good. We have to wait until full dark but let's have a look at the terrain.' They resumed their progress towards the back exit. 'There'll be some equipment coming in with an expert. Listening devices, heat contact gear.'

'He's here already,' the chief told Cowley. 'With my lads.'

As they left Cowley made a point of turning and waving. A woman police officer with the mother and child nodded, and the little girl waved back, very cheerfully, full of excitement.

With the feeling that at last things were moving along his way, Cowley went out and through the cinema car park. The feeling that they had unearthed the right house out of all the leads was strong on him. It might not be, of course; but it was all they had.

The local chief pointed. 'We can get through the bottom there, and then it's a hundred yards or so to the backway.'

Cowley surveyed the area, seeing the grimy houses, the lights speckling the dusk, itching for it to get dark so that they could get on with it. But he was intrigued.

'How,' he asked the chief: 'Just how did you spirit the neighbour and her little girl out of the house? They're tightly packed in.'

The local chief wanted to take pride in a good job well done.

'Sent one of our young woman constables in plain-clothes. The mother was agreeable – the only problem was to stop the kid from gawping at the suspect house.'

Cowley's smile switched on. 'How did they manage that?'

The local chief looked suitably modest.

'Bribery. The wonderful world of potato chips.'

Cowley shook his head at the infinite wonder of the world and then checked his watch. 'Be dark soon – and there's some cloud about, too.'

The wait, irksome though it was, passed at last and the night clamped down so that the CI5 men and police and listening experts could file silently and unseen through the darkness along the backway to the house next to the suspect house. Now Cowley felt even more sure this must be the one. Time, time, well, time was running out and yet if they hurried along and tipped their hand, made a mess of it – blood would flow and some of it would be Cowley's.

That his blood would be merely metaphorical, whilst that of Asher Biebermann's would drain his life away, was almost academic; a failure of this magnitude was tantamount to a death. And George Cowley was a man to whom life was precious. His own life and the lives of others . . .

Inside, the CI5 men cased the house. Single-parent families, despite Social Security, do not run to luxuries. The house was spick and span, clean, and showed marks of care. A discarded doll did not add a single note of untidiness. Rather, the doll complemented the appearance of the house, made it a home.

Bodie's pencil torch picked out the doll, lingered for a heartbeat, passed on. The kitchen table was set for an unfinished meal. Bread and jam, tea cups and saucers, a chocolate swiss roll already cut into slices. Cowley moved on towards the hall.

Throwing his torch beam ahead of Cowley, shedding a gaunt and demoniac shadow against the far wall, Bodie used his other hand to scoop up a cut slice of the chocolate swiss roll.

Moving like a tiger stalking its prey, Cowley ascended the stairs. One began to creak. Instantly, Cowley halted, his foot poised. Delicately, he let the offending stairtread settle into place, almost silently, and shifted his foot one tread higher. He went on, and his hand stabbed down, finger pointing at the treacherous step.

Throwing the light ahead, Bodie complied and stepped over the tread without stepping on it. Both men reached the upstairs landing.

The front bedroom possessed a feminine touch. On the wall the well-known picture of the Chinese Beauty glowed in blues and greens. A hairdryer and carmen rollers stood on the dressing table among bottles of perfume and hair lotions and the necessary adjuncts in a woman's life. The clutter was neatly arranged. Pink bedroom slippers, a pouffe, the wardrobe, all were normal for this sort of bedroom. The only sad note was struck by the bed, and that sadness would not be understood if you didn't know this was a single parent family. The bed was a double bed.

Cowley headed for the internal wall. He moved silently.

Softly, he said to Bodie: 'Get the boffin. And a decent light.'

Nodding, giving Cowley the torch, Bodie went out of that bedroom that told so much.

He went down the stairs with the same caution. In these houses they could hear you breathe next door. Wasn't there always arguments and bust-ups over the radio or TV being too loud? In the kitchen he used his handset and called Doyle.

'Doyle?'

'Yes?' Doyle's voice made Bodie jump, and he flapped his coat over the intercom.

'Send in the boffin. And a lamp.'

He switched off before Ray Doyle could bellow again.

Then, reflectively, he took another slice of the chocolate swiss roll.

Cowley came out on to the landing as the others came through the door. Bodie signalled the expert as they reached the creaky step. They started up again. Cowley abruptly lifted a hand, a commanding gesture that froze the others on the stairs.

Cowley put his ear to the wall.

A noise sounded, like a miniature Concorde taking off, a rumbling, rushing, whooshing sound, followed by the noise of a Niagara cascading. Someone had flushed a lavatory.

Cowley lowered his arm and gestured.

Bodie and the expert resumed their climb.

Amused, Bodie rubbed his stomach and whispered.

'Collywobbles . . . '

In the kidnap house Asher Biebermann lay sleeping heavily on his mattress on the floor. His gag had been removed; but he had been so deeply drugged he did not stir.

Mac, the third of the four kidnappers, entered the room, yawning and stretching, to take over the watch. A youngish man, his ferret-like face reflected the positive instincts in him, those of self-preservation, self-interest, and selfishness.

Frank stood up and twitched his machine pistol at the sleeping prisoner.

'He's well doped. But one bleat – use the chloroform!'

Mac nodded. It appeared he was not too displeased at the idea. Frank gave a yawn in turn and, after a final look at Biebermann, went out across the landing.

He went into the other bedroom where the table carried its freight of sharp and glittering surgeon's instruments.

Johnnie lay in his sleeping bag; but he was not asleep. The lantern at his side threw a sharp shadow like the Himalayas against the wall and the ex-army blanket covering the window.

With an uneasiness obvious from his voice, Johnnie said: 'They're moving about next door.'

'Why not?' said Frank. He felt weary. He sat at the table and began to pick at cheese and biscuits, casting crumbs in a yellow shower. 'It's not that late.'

'Did you hear them come back?'

'No.'

Johnnie frowned. 'Nor did I.'

Frank swallowed cheese and biscuits and, impatiently, said: 'So they came in the back.'

'Did the others hear them?'

Frank could feel the tiredness now and he was becoming exasperated. 'Go and ask 'em!'

Johnnie clumped up a chunk of his sleeping bag. 'Just checking. Just checking.'

Frank took another big bite and with his mouth full said: 'I wonder who the girl was? Haven't seen her around here before.'

'We've not been here that long – friend, sister, who knows? Good looking, though.'

'Yeah. When they've paid up and this lot is over . . .' He ran a hand along the machine pistol, and laughed.

'Sure,' said Johnnie. 'Come pay day . . .'

Next door in the neighbouring house the expert had his equipment set up and checked out and working perfectly. He listened intently, turning dials with long sensitive fingers. Presently, without speaking, he pointed at the wall. He held up three fingers, pointing. One, two, three. He indicated places. Cowley nodded, understanding. Three sources of noise, human noise . . .

'You,' Cowley told him, 'are in for a long night.'

The expert nodded, resigned, and then fished out his overnight bag and offered around sandwiches. Both Cowley and Bodie declined, gracefully.

So the night passed.

The sun rose nice and early, bright and polished, shining away as though nothing could be amiss with any world he shone on.

In the back garden the leaning wooden shed with a few panes of glass that might, once, have served as a surrogate greenhouse, smelled of the strange and jungly overnight aromas of the out-of-doors. That smell was strong even in a suburban London back garden.

Bodie pushed the door open on its one rusty hinge. He kept well away from any observation from the suspect house.

Looking in he saw the prostrate form in the anorak.

'Doyle!'

Doyle groaned. He turned over – painfully. A spider ran down out of his hair and ski-jumped off his nose.

He tried to ease himself to a more comfortable position and groaned again. He sat up, wincing, and then opened his eyes. He blinked at the strong sunshine.

'The old man's gone back to town,' said Bodie.

Doyle bashed dust from his anorak and looked not so much startled as fed up.

'Don't say we're up the wrong tree.'

'No. No, the Israelis have sussed we're on to something.'

Doyle stood up, almost braining himself on the low leaning roof. His curly hair was festooned with dust and cobwebs. He groaned and tried to stretch, and winced again.

'What do they want?' he demanded with disgust. 'Another Entebbe?'

Chapter Four

The Whitehall conference room was solid, impeccable as to taste and furnishing, the table gleaming, the chairs not too comfortable but not so uncomfortable as to be impolite. The few gilt-framed pictures represented resounding British triumphs of a past in which scarlet coats and Brown Besses roared on to inevitable victory.

Hirschfield, the Israeli Embassy official, and the Minister sat in apparent ease. George Cowley also sat and his ease reflected the tearing impatience in him to get back to the suspect house. But this confrontation was overdue and could not be ignored. On this kind of conference and the impression he created lay the mark British Security would make on world opinion.

Hirschfield knew exactly what he was about, and he spoke with a little irony not lost on the others. 'The whole world knows – your policemen are wonderful.'

Very carefully, Cowley said: 'If you want to know the time – '

'Exactly, Mr Cowley, you are an elusive man. You left central London last evening – '

'Oh.' Cowley looked almost genuinely surprised. 'Those were your people.'

'Yes,' said Hirschfield. He was put out but he betrayed nothing. 'They were intercepted by a police patrol, and told, most politely, that they were exceeding the speed limit.'

The Minister leaned forward. He was mildly amused at the fencing going on. 'Even with diplomatic plates, one is expected to conform with the laws of the land.'

'Of course.' Hirschfield waved the irritation away. His people had tried one trick, it had failed, now he would press that much harder. 'You have some definite information?'

'Let's just say,' said Cowley, 'we are pursuing a promising line of enquiry.'

Now Hirschfield turned a sterner gaze on the chief of CI5.

'Can we be of assistance?'

Cowley drew a breath. The answer he had to give was the right one. He did not look at the Minister as he spoke.

'At this stage – I think not. What about our Arab friend's proposal?'

Hirschfield put on his face what passed for a wry smile.

'Such generosity. With friends like that, who needs enemies?'

'It seemed – plausible. Might not something – '

'But it hasn't come to that, yet.' Hirschfield got back to his main preoccupation. 'This "promising line" as you call it. I do think, diplomatically speaking you understand, that we are, er, entitled to, er, detailed information.'

'The diplomacy you speak of is outside my particular province. Obviously, if I were instructed to amplify the information, I would do so.' That, thought George Cowley, should deal with that one rather nicely. He cocked an eye at the Minister. 'Minister?'

This hot potato was fielded easily and returned like a ball from first base. 'I really think Mr Cowley knows what he is doing.'

Hirschfield was forced to acknowledge the point. So, he went on with his programme. 'Sir. We have had, sad to say, a lot of experience in this kind of thing.'

'Yes,' said the Minister. 'I know.' The genuineness of his words was unmistakable.

Cowley cut in. 'If he's where we think he is, we'll get him back for you.'

With a bitterness that, however justified it was, Hirschfield deplored in himself, he said grittily: 'Dead or alive . . . '

Cowley braced up.
'Alive, I hope.'

Ray Doyle was an ex-copper and this caper he was on now was right back in the days of trailing villains around the open haunts of London where their villainy thrived. At least, he had Sally Lawford at the wheel of the squad car to keep him company.

Sally was a dish, and that, in these circumstances, was a bit of a problem. She wore sensible shoes, and a skirt, and a blouse that had frills enough to disguise the shape that could have launched a thousand and a half ships. She made herself look inconspicuous, and that was enough of a success to make Doyle imagine she'd be first rate. Of course, Cowley would never had allowed Sally Lawford to associate with CI5 if she couldn't handle herself . . .

They watched from the corner as Frank let himself out of the suspect house. He took a swift glance up and down the street, and then walked off. He moved aggressively, shoulders hunched; but wisps of tiredness clung to him. Doyle spoke into the car radio mike.

'Yes. Seen him.'

He alighted from the car and smiled at Sally. She waited the regulation time before carefully tooling the dark blue car out into the road and following on. Doyle tailed with the skill and professional competence his training as a detective had given him, allied to the natural flair he possessed. Being in CI5 sharpened up a man's wits no end. Frank walked into the underground station and, after a decent interval for tickets, Doyle followed.

Frank bought a newspaper and Doyle, waiting and watching, moved smoothly into line. A few stops along Frank alighted. He dumped the paper in a waste basket. Doyle let Frank get well ahead and then called through on his handset, giving details and locations. He wanted back up, if he wanted it, damned quick.

The way Doyle figured what Frank was up to went something after the fashion that Frank knew pretty well what he was about, having no idea at all that the house in which he had spent the night was under observation; but that he wanted to lay a false trail so that when, as eventually he must, he completed what he had come out for, the witnesses to his presence would be non-existent. That, it seemed to Doyle, could be the only explanation for this nonsensical traipsing about, for now Frank boarded a bus, and jumped off at full tilt a few stops along. Doyle did a quick recovery on that one, calling in Sally who had followed along the underground line by surface road. The kidnappers had called up before from a local box and been sharp enough to ring off before the line could be traced. So why all this malarkey, acting like Dick Barton?

This time when Frank went into a shopping precinct, bought two papers and then entered a phone box, it was Sally's turn to keep close obbo on him. Doyle stayed in the car.

The kidnapper dialled out, checking from one of the papers he had. Sally pottered about in the nearest shop, a chemists, whilst appearing to examine sunglasses, post-cards, tubes of toothpaste. She did a nice job of it. Frank in the phone box completed his call and elbowed his way out of the box.

When Sally joined him in the car, Doyle just hoped that the kidnapper's mystery tour was over.

The Asian cinema car park had been turned into a species of battle headquarters. But everything was low key and no one would suspect anything was going on. A large lorry drove into the car park with its superstructure covered by a new bright green tarpaulin. A man wearing a welder's helmet tipped back signalled to the lorry driver where to pull up.

Watching them from the side, Bodie went on speaking into his handset.

'You've got to hand it to them. They've got a sense of humour.' The lorry stopped and the engine cut. Bodie looked up and said to the welder: 'Make it strong. I don't want my head knocked off.' Then, back to his radio, speaking to his partner, he went on: 'They called the *Sporting Life*!'

In the car Doyle reacted to the news. The kidnapper had bought more than one paper and he could have phoned any newsdesk. The *Sporting Life* seemed ironical enough to liven a villain's day. 'Well,' Doyle gave his opinion over the radio. 'They're taking a gamble.'

'Touché.' Bodie let a smile lift those mobile lips, 'They want the jackpot.'

'How much?'

'Two million. Half a million apiece.'

Doyle lifted his eyebrows at Sally.

'Is that all?'

Bodie's voice catalogued the kidnappers' demands.

'A military aircraft fuelled for three thousand miles. Twelve – repeat twelve – parachutes. And the money, of course.'

Both partners recognised the brains at work behind these demands. It was Doyle who said: 'They've got their own pilot. The RAF crew jump first, right?'

'Right!' said Bodie, watching the welder fussing with his equipment. 'If anyone fancies tampering with the parachutes – well, it would be a touch of the old Russian Roulette.'

Doyle said: 'Nice one.'

They finished up the radio conversation with Doyle saying a tail was still on the kidnapper and that he was coming back to the car park. Bodie stuck his head under the green tarpaulin, and drew his cheeks in, whistling silently, his dark eyes thoughtful.

When Doyle drew into the car park he pulled in alongside the white Rover 3500. He started to alight, then paused and turned back, leaning across the seats. Sally looked up, and if she guessed what he was going to do she made no move – either way. The kiss Doyle placed delicately on her smooth cheek was a mere peck. But it was a peck of first quality.

'Your clutch is slipping.'

Sally smiled. 'My clutch – or my touch?'

Doyle smiled back. 'All we need is the time and place.'

'You're as bad as Bodie.'

'As bad – or as good?'

Walking away with a barely discernible swagger to his anoraked shoulders, Doyle mentally chalked up another future opening. Sally moved across to the driving seat and started to check her immaculate makeup.

Great events are often begun by the smallest of incidents, tiny happenstances that seem trivial at the time. Snug in his place of concealment, Cowley scrutinised the suspect house through binoculars. Abruptly he focused intently. He froze. Then he let out a gust of disgusted breath. 'That's all we need!'

At his side the local chief stiffened. 'What's that, sir?'

'The child. The neighbour's child. They've let her through.'

'The school.' The chief checked his watch. He felt the bile rising. 'It's just after twelve...'

Into the back garden the girl led her companion, her best friend, Julie, whom she loved and hated by turns, as one should a best friend. They were dressed in exactly the same school uniform and they giggled as they approached the wired rabbit hutches by the leaning shed where Doyle had spent the night.

Taking food from the bin the girl said: 'Poor Thumper must be *starving*.' The rabbit food splayed out on to the dish in the straw and the rabbit, who had been standing up on her hind legs pawing at the wire, dived in with a quivering eagerness. Julie glanced up at the next door house. 'That's where those men are. Mum says they're bad men, they've done something terrible . . . ' Both schoolgirls looked up in fearful expectation at the suspect house.

From the upper window Johnnie looked out and saw the two girls in the next door garden fiddling around at the rabbit hutch. They were looking up at the window and instinctively he drew back. He felt worried. He didn't know what was happening. From his angle he saw Frank come walking up the backway to the garden. Galvanised by a sense of urgency, Johnnie rapped on the window.

The girls saw the big man walking into the next door garden, and they heard the sharp rap, like hailstones, on the window.

Frank stopped.

He looked swiftly at the upper window, seeing Johnnie lurking beyond the panes.

He swung about and stared at the two little girls.

A piece of lettuce, carefully hoarded for Thumper, floated to the ground.

For a moment the tension stretched . . .

Frank began to move again and the two girls came back to life.

'Come on ! Let's run for it !'

Together, their legs flashing, the girls ran out of the garden.

Frank and Johnnie stared after them until they were lost to view.

Then, moving with a determination that turned his face into a savage mask, Frank ran full tilt through the back door into the house.

Very little luck had been involved in the successful tracking down of the kidnappers of Asher Biebermann. Certainly, Cowley considered, the villains had been a mite careless in allowing more into the Polaroid picture than they should have. But that was a villain's mistake, and not a raw slice of luck for CI5. Painstaking work had resulted in the discovery of the correct house. The details in the picture had been found and matched with the site. And now – this !

In the neighbour's house the listening expert put his half-eaten sandwich down quickly, spilling liver sausage from the butter-limp bread.

He listened. His sensitive equipment picked up sounds; but his expertise sorted them out and gave them meaning. He snapped his fingers.

The big bulky man in the shooting-jacket with the brown lace-up boots and cords half-turned from his observation from the window. Neatly arranged lay a Lee Enfield .303 with scoped sights. The marksman trusted that old bondouk over and above all your fancy FNs. With his middle finger on the trigger and his forefinger and thumb working the bolt he could let off ten of the best in lightning-time.

The listening expert called across to the marksman.

'There's something up! They're buzzing around like flies.'

Instantly the marksman picked up the handset and called out.

'Red Zed. They're on the move!'

He put the handset down and reached for the Lee Enfield.

Taking the call, feeling that out of disaster must come forth goodness, Cowley gave his orders and triggered the action.

'Bodie!' He spoke with the full knowledge that however good his men were, the final responsibility was down to him. 'Bodie – you're on!'

Four armed men in the house, and a bound prisoner in the upper bedroom – the fortress was a sticky one for the agents of CI5. Cowley and his men had planned. The welder had finished his job. Now it remained to be seen if the plan would work.

Dead or Alive – both sides had used that expression . . .

Ray Doyle headed along the backway, his Browning auto in his fist, his body bent double to give him as much concealment as possible. The big hit would be made by Bodie . . .

Bodie crouched in the jerry-built structure welded on the lorry. The steel beams surrounded him, hard and ugly. The green canvas had been thrown back to reveal the superstructure, the projecting battering ram and the shield which – so it was devoutly believed – would afford him protection from machine pistol fire.

The lorry picked up speed heading down the street. It ground through the gears, the engine note rising higher and higher, growling like a beast in a cage hurling itself at the iron bars. The lorry belted along, swaying, the welded superstructure and Bodie jolting along like maniacal surf-boarders.

At precisely the right moment the lorry swerved hard, jolted up over the pavement, headed straight at the kidnap house.

The steel battering ram crashed stunningly through the window.

Glass and sashes sprayed, the curtains flapped wildly.

Bodie was catapulted forward. There was almost no need to jump, the violence of the crash flinging him headlong through the cross-bracing of the superstructure and up and over the shield. He sailed through the ruins of the window. The noise continued to boom and baroom around in his skull; but he hit the floor on his feet, like a cat.

The kidnapper in the room jerked up, startled out of his wits by the massive steel snout poking like an aircraft crash through the window, by the shrapnel spray of glass and, last and possibly by far the worst, the appearance of a man like a demon from a stage trapdoor. The demon triggered a burst from his Browning auto and the kidnapper shrieked as the slugs bit into him. He had had time to snatch up his machine pistol. But his forefinger contracted on the trigger as the gun pointed to the sky and the bullets stitched patterns in the ceiling.

Bodie went on forward, kicked the kidnapper as he went down and grabbed the gun away from nerveless fingers.

With the uproar of that smash still ringing on the air Doyle kicked the back door open and belted in, his gun ready.

At the window of the next door house the marksmen lifted the sash and leaned out. A man appeared at the back window, popping out just as Doyle went in below. The marksman had time for a single shot which drove Mac, the kidnapper, back inside the house.

Johnnie heard the uproar, the colossal smash, the ringing bursts of gunfire. He ran crazily along the landing, ignoring the bedrooms, started down the stairs. He held his machine pistol up and his hands shook on the cold metal.

Charging in through the kicked-open back door Doyle spotted the man on the stairs, saw the ugly machine pistol, let fly with a burst of aimed shots. Johnnie had no time to scream. He was cut down, blood spouting, toppled over the banisters, the machine pistol flying up and crashing on to the corridor. Johnnie glimpsed a fading vision of hot sun-kissed beaches, of birds who would never be hotly-kissed by him, and then he thudded on to the floor.

Up in the bathroom Frank smashed out of the door and on to the landing. The whole house shuddered to noise. The hullaballoo was like that of an upturned beehive. Bodie belted out of the bedroom just as Frank emerged from the bathroom.

The confrontation held for a heartbeat.

Bodie's gun belched flame. The slug hit Frank in the hand that gripped his gun and Frank shrieked with the sudden stinging pain. He dropped his machine pistol. Bodie stalked across.

'More?'

Frank shook his head, gasping, and sank to his knees. He clung on to his hand which felt as though he'd caught it in a white-hot press and then dunked it in a pail of ice.

But Mac, who had taken chips of brick on his face so that drops of blood caught in the bristles of his beard like rubies, burst from the back bedroom. Bodie stood facing Frank, his back to Mac. The kidnapper swung his gun up, determined to shoot one of the bastards.

A shot belched.

Mac's finger loosened on the trigger. He looked utterly surprised.

Bodie turned.

He looked down the stairwell.

Doyle stood there, his Browning still snouting up uglily, his face, round and fierce, staring up. He was still in the regulation shooting pose.

Perfectly composed, Bodie said: 'What kept you?'

Then they carried out checks, Doyle below stairs, with

Bodie hurrying back to the front bedroom where the monstrous steel battering ram stuck jaggedly in through the ruined window. As other CI5 men moved in with ready handcuffs, Bodie stowed his auto away and knelt beside Asher Biebermann. He gently undid the blindfold and removed it and then the gag.

'Shalom, sir,' said Bodie, keeping it very cool.

The Israeli Cabinet Minister gasped for breath – and then he was once more in control.

'Shabbat Shalom.'

Brodie looked blank.

Biebermann summoned up a weary smile.

'It is Friday, isn't it? The start of our Sabbath.'

Bodie smiled that famous smile. 'Yes, of course. Well, if you're going to the synagogue, say one for me.'

Doyle walked in and he was smiling, too. It had gone like a pound of butter down the chute – smooth.

'And me, sir.' Then, to Bodie: 'Did you bring his shoe?'

That creased Bodie up.

But, up the stairs bellowed a ferocious voice.

'Doyle! Bodie! Where are you?'

That furious voice was followed instantly by George Cowley, gun in hand, erupting into the room. He stopped stock still. He saw his two alleged top agents. He saw the rescued Israeli Cabinet Minister. He saw everything.

'Oh, good afternoon, sir,' said the Chief of CI5. 'I trust I find you well . . . '

When all the political ramifications had been neatly tidied up and the de-briefing of the operation had brought to light strengths and weaknesses, Cowley, Doyle and Bodie went to see about what some people would call more important matters. They were invited to tea with the divorced lady and her little girl in the neighbour-house to what had been the kidnap house, and they went conscious of the importance of the occasion to the woman and her daughter.

The whole house had been tidied to a new height of

neatness and the kitchen positively gleamed in spick-and-span freshness.

On the table covered by a pretty floral tablecloth had been set out the best china. Matching plates lay empty and waiting for the contents of the paper bag in the hand of the little girl as she ran in from the bakers.

The lady was saying: 'I'm afraid it's only Indian, Mr Cowley.'

'It's perfect – very welcome, I assure you.'

Then the girl could not be contained any longer.

'Currant loaf, Mum, and a chocolate swiss role.'

Cowley, sauvely, said: 'That's something else we must indent for. One swiss roll.' He half-glanced at Bodie, who looked smug and then lifted his eyebrows at Cowley's words. 'Bodie here is still a growing lad.'

Slices were soon cut off and the lady said: 'He looks as if he has a healthy appetite. And what about you, Mr Doyle?'

'Oh,' said Ray Doyle comfortably. 'I'll stick with the currant loaf. The swiss roll's a bit heady for me.'

Bodie took an immense bite from the swiss roll and winked at the girl. Old Ray Doyle could always put in the elbow; but the Aylesbury Duck needed a lot of beating, at that . . .

Chapter Five

The strong-boned, bristle-haired, clean-cut young man acted as a fugitive would act. Cautiously he peered from the sagging window with its jagged edges of shattered glass at the hunters who searched, patiently and methodically, through the ugly area of derelict buildings.

The hunters all wore flak-jackets over their civilian clothes, and bulky, visored helmets. They moved with the sure purpose of men who have done this before, and know how to do it. They would flush the quarry, bring him yelling into the open. And then . . .

The naked buildings with their ages-old patina of grime and their crumbling brickwork would muffle the yells. The leaning walls seemed to shut off the sky. The fugitive left the crazy concealment of the window and, crouched double, made for the rotten stairs to the roof. Up there, he could dodge between two buildings and gain the far roof, and, perhaps, safety . . .

Half a mile away George Cowley nestled at the sight of a streamlined automatic weapon, his eye cuddling the plastic-cup of the scope. A bullet-shaped pod mounted with the scope lent a vague air of futuristic weaponry to the automatic rifle cum submachinegun. Carefully, easily, Cowley lined up the sights.

The fugitive reached the edge of the roof. A red spot appeared near him on the stairhead. It shifted across but the fugitive moved away, heading along the crumbled roof edge. The red spot tracked him.

In the littered area below with splintered beams and the detritus of fallen bricks the hunters moved in with sure purpose. The fugitive took one look and moved hastily away to his side, crouched, moving away from that rubble-strewn area.

He poised for the leap on to the adjoining roof where he could slide into the shadows and lose himself. He took a deep breath, and revealed a fine physique, strained now to the utmost. His legs braced.

The red spot jumped into life on his forehead.

The fugitive pumped power into his legs and swung his arms forward ready to leap and the red spot shone full in his eyes.

Dazzled, his leap went haywire. In a tumbled sprawl of arms and legs he toppled from the roof and plummeted down through the air.

Down he fell, twisting over like a rag doll splashed back-first into a wide tank of water. Spray festooned out like lace. Gasping and spluttering, red-faced, the fugitive surfaced and paddled to the metal edge of the tank.

The hunters in their flak-jackets and helmets waited for him . . .

George Cowley took the smg from his shoulder and stood up from his firing position. Doyle and Bodie rose to stand beside him. Their expressions were neutral; but their thoughts buzzed.

'Sloppy!' said Cowley, with the snap of decision.

'But,' said Bodie. 'The poor bastard's half a mile away, on another course.'

'His mistake.' Cowley knew these two were aware he was riding a hobby-horse; but he didn't care. You were never too old or too good to learn – or be reminded. 'Assuming the only enemy is the one you can see.' He snapped the gun into both capable fists and then thrust it like a quarterstave at Doyle. 'Laserlock sight. Try it!'

The training area was a wilderness of brick and stone, of splintered wood and barbed wire and old tin cans. Stray cats would have found it a heaven, if they could have suffered the noise of gunfire. A larger building, ancient like everything else around this discarded section of the city, rose some way off, its Gothic architecture and enamelled tiles grotesque in the surrounding desolation.

From the rubble a man-sized and man-shaped target abruptly popped up into view. Cowley gave his orders over his handset with great relish, and the target-operators followed suit with equal delight. They took a pride in their work, and their job was to make hell for every man – or woman – who set foot in here thinking that CI5 was a soft option.

Doyle swung and the red spot appeared over the heart of the target and the burst of auto fire ripped the heart area to shreds.

Other targets popped up, at succeedingly increased distances, and Ray Doyle swung with them. The red dot smoked up on each target and was followed at once by the unerring thunk of a bullet striking home. As Cowley and Bodie watched, Doyle finished the display by a long raking burst which slashed across a row of targets, decapitating them.

Cowley nodded. 'Very impressive.'

Doyle said: 'Couldn't miss.'

Bodie said: 'Nobody could.'

Doyle started to say: 'Thanks –'

And Bodie went on: 'Not under those conditions.'

So Doyle finished tartly: ' – friend.'

They stood for a moment glaring at each other, the smg between them. Cowley was already marching off. Doyle with the gun swung away to follow him, still feeling the impressive power and accuracy of the smg. Bodie stood where he was and his lips wrinkled and his eyebrows drew down.

Cowley did not turn but waved an imperious arm. 'Come.'

'Don't I get a turn?' There was no mistaking the hurt in Bodie's voice.

Cowley half-turned. 'It is not a toy, Bodie.'

Fed-up but knowing when to use his head, Bodie tagged along. 'No, sir,' he said. It did not seem as though it was going to be one of his better days.

On their way into the action-course HQ they passed the

fugitive. Soaking wet, glowering, he trudged along – squelching.

As they passed Cowley spoke as though to no one in particular, an airy observation at random. 'Seems to have been raining.'

Well, Bodie reflected, as he dutifully said: 'Yes, sir,' that made up a little . . .

Cowley got down to business.

'So,' he said, still moving, energetic, filled with the drive that forced success from seemingly inevitable disaster. 'The 180 submachinegun. You like it?'

'Like?' said Doyle, by his tone conveying something of the feelings he'd expected shooting the 180.

Bodie said bluntly: 'It's lethal.'

In his dry way, Cowley said: 'Guns are.' They were passing an area in which trainees were being flushed out of ruined cellars by smoke grenades and not much liking it. Cowley took absolutely no notice of the bangs or the smoke. 'The 180 is the very latest thing in American weaponry. Laserlock sight.'

'Range?'

'Effective up to a thousand yards. At least.'

'The red dot?' said Bodie, keeping up with the others.

'From the laser,' Cowley told him. 'Is all the aiming you need. Where the red dot is, the bullets strike.' They neared the Gothic building and the bangs diminished to their rear. 'Ammunition, point two two calibre. Automatic, repeating or single shot.'

'Hits without fail?' said Doyle.

'Rate of fire?' said Bodie.

'So they claim. On automatic, 900 rounds a minute.'

Doyle could work that one. 'Fifteen rounds a second.'

They moved up the ancient steps of the building towards doors that appeared almost to be falling off their hinges. There were other doors at the back of these. 'They claim it can cut down telegraph poles.'

Bodie said: 'Nice.'

Doyle said: 'Nasty.'

The Gothic building into which they walked with that

brisk, energetic bustle about every movement was an ancient tiled municipal swimming pool with baths attached. It served as the action-course HQ admirably. At the moment, although the pool was full, no swimmers disturbed the water which lapped against the tiles and set up that hollow cavernous echo that seemed to swirl physically in the air and twine right through the ears and into the guts. The three men made their way along the tiled edge of the pool past the closed doors of changing stalls.

At the far end by the door leading off into the superintendent's offices a smartly dressed and attractive girl stood waiting. Kathie had been waiting for some time and was accustomed to that boredom in life. Her slight nervousness was well masked. Attractive, with a neatness about her and a competence that came from self-knowledge, she looked to be about twenty-eight, and was a girl at whom men would look twice.

Fastened to the wall at the side of the door to the superintendent's office a full-length mirror caught some of the water-reflections from the roof and changed colour and shade confusingly. Kathie did not look at the mirror.

As the men came in, Bodie was saying: 'The laser sight could give your position away.'

'It might.' Cowley remembered the confused look on the tough face of the agent training as a CI5 man when he'd toppled off the roof. 'But it can also dazzle and so temporarily blind an enemy.'

'Temporarily . . .' said Doyle.

Cowley bustled past Kathie completely ignoring her, heading for the super's office. Bodie, being Bodie, tried a big come-on smile. He got nowhere, which more surprised than hurt him. Following the other two, Doyle saw Kathie.

For an instant their eyes met.

Luckily – so Doyle considered – neither Cowley nor Bodie observed that swift and as swiftly-hidden flash of recognition. His face set, Doyle marched past Kathie and followed the others through into the office.

He closed the door carefully after them.

Ruth, Cowley's current personal assistant, stood by the

wall, looking through the full-length two-way mirror at Kathie. Ruth was, as was proper, a stunner. She wore clothes that would have been out of place in the derelict area – a trim pleated skirt and blouse – her hair immaculate, her face intent with her perfectly-shaped lips half-parted. But Ruth would have made those clothes perfect for wherever she happened to be. She pressed the release button on the video camera mounted on a tripod and the camera stopped whirring. It had been recording all Kathie's movements faithfully, and subsequently that record would be used in the evaluation in which Kathie would or would not be judged fit to join CI5.

Cowley nodded to Ruth, who smiled and exited through the inner door. She most carefully – most carefully indeed – did not so much as look or acknowledge the presence of Bodie.

As for Bodie, he stared through the two-way mirror. His face held a lively admiration.

'Nice. That's no scrubber.'

'No,' said Doyle, rather sharply, putting an edge to the jokey remark. 'Not your type at all.'

With an air of immense patience, Cowley said: 'If you've quite finished . . . '

Bodie said: 'A healthy interest, sir.'

Doyle said: 'A natural obsession, that's all.'

'In that case, you wouldn't want me to keep the young lady waiting.'

'First interview, is it, sir?'

'What's that to you, Doyle?'

The pause before Doyle answered was barely perceptible.

Then: 'Nothing, sir.' Ray Doyle's voice was neutral.

Bodie butted in, anxious to get on. 'Are we buying the gun, sir?'

'That's up to you two.'

'Us, sir?'

'As of now, you're both suspended from other duties. Take that gun and test it. I want to know every advantage and every weakness. I want to know exactly how useful it could be – to us. And exactly how dangerous it could be if used against us.'

Doyle shook his head. 'That I wouldn't fancy.'

'Good.' Cowley took great pleasure in throwing the 180 at Doyle, who caught it with casual expertise. 'In that case, you'll look after it, won't you, Doyle?'

And Cowley strode off back through the doorway into the swimming pool area. He said over his shoulder: 'Guard it, Doyle. Guard it with your life. In the wrong hands that gun could create an instant disaster area. Anywhere.'

'Thank you, sir,' said Doyle in a highly doubtful tone.

Bodie, feeling left out – again – said: 'Ammunition?'

Cowley pointed to a holdall on the table. 'Ammunition.'

The door swung to after him.

Bodie and Doyle regarded each other with a dryness that came from an understanding of what they had been landed with. Taking the 180 from his partner, Bodie lifted it and aimed through the two-way mirror. The red spot centred first on Kathie and then on Cowley as the pair moved away along the tiled pool edge. Bodie was far too much of a professional to take off the safety – especially with a gun like this.

As he aimed the smg Bodie said in a mock-gruff voice, breaking up the words: 'Guard-it-with-your-life . . . In the wrong hands it could . . . create an – instant disaster area . . .'

A loud and clacking click of a relay closing snapped through the room. The image in the two-way mirror vanished. Bodie swung around with the 180 pointed.

At the inner door Ruth looked startled. On that immaculate white blouse of hers a red spot glowed.

Relaxing and going towards the other door, Ruth spoke with a little tartness.

'Hadn't you two better go and do whatever it is you're supposed to be doing?'

Cowley's personal assistant for the moment looked through the two-way mirror observing her boss talking with Miss

Mason. Ruth held her clipboard and a stopwatch, and a tiny frown dinted in between her eyebrows. If she thought about Bodie at all, she reminded herself very firmly not to think about him. Not at all.

Cowley was saying: 'Thank you, Miss Mason. We'll be in touch in a few days.'

He stood for a moment watching as Kathie walked off and then he went into the super's office, and stood beside Ruth still watching as Kathie Mason left the swimming pool.

'Well?'

'Reaction,' said Ruth. 'Good.'

Considering carefully, Cowley switched off the mirror. Then he made up his mind. 'Organise a full screening of our Miss Mason. Blue list.'

'Yes, sir,' said Ruth and took her stopwatch, her clipboard and her stunning self off to her own office.

Outside in the car park only Doyle's car and Cowley's were parked up near the office. The sky looked set to be clear for a space; but that wasn't the reason Ray Doyle took the light weight golf bag from the back. As Bodie watched, Doyle stowed the 180 smg away in the golf bag. Doyle looked up.

'You want to get in the back?'

'What should I want to get in the back for?'

Doyle smiled. 'Keep an eye on the gun. And leave the front free for Miss Mason.'

'What makes you think,' demanded Bodie, belligerently, 'she'll want to get in?'

Doyle looked across at the exit door as Kathie Mason came out. Bodie's mobile lips wrinkled up. Well . . . He sat in the back of the car prepared to see his oppo Ray Doyle cut down to size. The girl walked straight towards the car. Doyle opened the front passenger door for her. Kathie got in.

Bodie gaped.

Doyle, getting in his side, jerked his head. 'That's Bodie.'

With vast composure, Kathie said: 'Hello, Bodie.'

That young man managed to get out: 'Miss Mason –'

Doyle, enjoying himself, said: 'We're giving him a lift.'

Bodie struggled to surface. 'Only if you're going my way.'

'Then tea?' Doyle made the question an invitation.

'Fine by me,' Bodie said, sitting back. 'How about you?'

Kathie smiled in reply. Doyle started the car and they moved off with the tyres crunching over the odd spot of rubble.

'I take it,' Bodie said with an aloof air, 'you two've known each other a long time.' At Kathie's nod he went on: 'Then you know one thing. Doyle never drinks anything but Lapson Souchong.'

Doyle's car trundled out of the car park and picked up speed along the road. Over beyond another stretch of waste ground – innocent waste ground – a dark Porsche started up. The foreign car bumped awkwardly over the rubble and bricks and swung into the road and followed Doyle's car. It followed discreetly and at a serviceable distance.

In the back seat Bodie unzipped the lightweight golf bag and took out the 180. He held it, not so much lovingly as with the appreciative professional grip of a man completely at home with firearms. Kathie glanced back.

'What's that for?'

'He's taking it home,' said Bodie, casually. 'He needs some extra coaching.' He leaned forward. 'You two haven't met before by any chance.' As Doyle and Kathie exchanged smiles, he said, a mite disgruntled. 'Or am I being obvious?'

'Well, not for a couple of years . . .'

'At the Yard,' said Doyle. 'Kathie's in C 11. Intelligence.'

'Why you looking for a transfer then?'

'To be near me.' Doyle liked the sound of that one.

'Partly,' said Kathie. 'I thought it would be a good way to work off my paranoia.'

'Oh yeah,' said Bodie. 'What's that?'

'An expensive way of hating somebody,' said Doyle. He

was watching his mirror with an alert, poised air. Bodie spotted that alertness in his partner, and felt the tingle over his body.

'We got a problem?' As he spoke, Bodie knew they had.

'Maybe . . . I think we might have a tail.'

Doyle tooled his car along at a regulation speed and picked up the blue signs indicating a dual carriageway ahead.

Bodie looked back through the rear window. 'The Porsche?' He patted the smg. 'Want to give him a blast?'

'Slice him in two.' Doyle swung the car into the access road. 'That'd give him a surprise.'

Bodie saw the way his partner was going. 'Try him out?'

Doyle nodded. 'Dummy. Hold tight.'

On the dual carriageway, which was only light with traffic, Doyle abruptly hit the accelerator. His dark blue car responded and hurtled ahead. The passing scenery blurred.

The Porsche responded, howling along in pursuit.

The signs for a flyover and exit ramps showed, swirling towards them. Bodie said: 'He's sticking . . .'

Without wasting a word or a movement Doyle spun his car sharp left-handed into the exit ramp and stamped on the brakes as the corner came up. The car howled around the curve, losing speed dramatically, straightening out. The Porsche went sailing on over the flyover. Feeling like a formula one driver Doyle swung the car around the curve and shot up on to the access ramp, back on to the dual carriageway and fell in neatly behind the Porsche. They could not make out any details of the driver. The two cars roared on, as though glued together.

A roundabout showed ahead and rapidly swung nearer. The Porsche went around, leaning, tyres squealing, spitting stones. Doyle followed.

Around they went and back again.

Bodie said: 'Ease up, then . . .'

Doyle eased the pressure of his right foot and the Porsche, going on around the roundabout, snaked up behind them. They took the exit and motored along the dual carriageway again.

Then, completely surprising the partners, the Porsche speeded up. The foreign car passed relatively smoothly. As it went by the driver tooted his horn. He waved. The movement was a mere lifting of the arm, a vague signal, but the gesture prevented either Doyle or Bodie getting a good view of the driver's face. The Porsche speeded on ahead.

Bodie let his breath out. 'Always wanted to be a racing driver.'

Doyle shook his head, letting his car tool along smoothly. 'Shame to spoil his fun.'

Kathie sat back. 'Are you two always like this?'

With a mock seriousness, Bodie told her. 'No. Sometimes we imagine people are following us. Tea?'

'My place or yours?' said Doyle.

'Yours.'

Doyle said: 'Shut up, Bodie.'

'Where are we going, then?'

It was left to Kathie, impishly, to say: 'His place.'

The dark Porsche waited almost out of sight around the corner from Doyle's flat. Doyle was enough of a professional to be able to spot a car with which he'd had a pleasant if minor argy-bargy along the dual carriageway. So the car snouted discreetly, parked with others, undistinguished.

Doyle, Bodie and Kathie drove up, still talking, still between them getting Bodie going and making sure Bodie knew it. Doyle pulled up and set the handbrake. He opened his side door and got out and then, gallantly, went around to open Kathie's. Bodie had to do for himself. They were all out of the car, waiting for Doyle to find his front door keys.

From the Porsche's side window the snout of a long and extremely high-power telescopic lens protruded. There were three distinct and separate sliding clatters of a focal plane shutter.

Three photographs were made, one, two, three, Kathie, Bodie, Doyle.

Doyle.

He was the one the photograph showed carrying a lightweight golf bag over his shoulder.

Relishing their opportunity to use the full resources afforded them by CI5 and the Army and Navy and Air Force, the partners put the new 180 smg through its paces.

Strapped in alongside the pilot of a helicopter, Doyle used the gun over the Army's Air Corps ranges, shooting the hell out of targets, getting the red spot zeroed in and then blasting away.

Over the tank training ranges – weirdly devilish landscapes of traps and snares – the gun was cradled by Bodie, riding a Land-Rover with a CI5 agent driving. Bright blue balloons trailed skywards. Bodie's first shot burst the first, and instantly another appeared lifting up. Before the blue balloon reached the end of its tether it was blown to shreds. And the next. And the next.

The Navy chipped in with a speedboat which crested the waves and leaped and bucked like the most savage unbroken bronco the old west had ever known. Leaping and surging, the speedboat roared across the lumpy water. And blue balloon after blue balloon floated up in swift succession to be blown into tatters against the sky.

The big cylinder had once been polished and shiny; but years of work had dulled it to a rich ochre colour. Sand drifted. The cylinder revolved briskly at the end of the open shed. The moment it stopped the tech flipped the latches and the cylinder parted along the joins like a para container. Doyle raked in among the sand and hauled out the 180 smg.

Without even blowing the sand away he whipped the gun up and pressed the trigger.

The 180 broke into a staccato burst of fire, instantly, perfectly.

There were rifles the Americans would never allow through the sand test. This new one, the 180 smg, handled the sand test as though it was best quality rifle oil.

Bodie dug the gun out of a trench filled with liquid mud and shot her off, perfectly. The laserlock sight functioned without a hitch.

Working with the technical experts they evaluated the parameters that would be of importance in the job. Not so much muzzle velocity or terminal velocity or even foot-pounds of power, so much as what the gun would actually do in combat.

Oak boards, steel plate, wadges of sacking, were shot through until the limits were reached. Those limits were way out, and represented highly impressive performance characteristics.

The testing took time but they worked their way through with determination and a growing respect for the 180.

Feeling they had done a good job they rendezvoused at Doyle's flat, prepared to go out on the tiles, as the wags once had it, and enjoy themselves. They still wore the combat fatigues they'd worn during their strenuous bouts of testing and the mud, sand, grit and muck added to the camouflage.

Doyle carried the 180 and Bodie the ammunition – what there was left of it.

The built-in cupboard on an inside wall looked innocent enough. Doyle led the way across. He fished out a chain which hung around his neck and down inside his shirt, and pulled out the key. With this key he unlocked the cupboard. Each man put in his burden; Doyle stowed the smg away and Bodie stacked the ammo. Then Doyle closed the cupboard, locked it, and let the key and chain drop down into his shirt.

That, then, was that . . .

Crossing to Doyle's sideboard to pour himself a drink, Bodie said: 'Nice day's shooting. Pity it's not the grouse season.'

Doyle's mouth curved down. 'With the 180? All you'd be left with is a handful of feathers.' He patted the key under his shirt. 'Check?'

'Check. I could do with a bath.'

Wrinkling up his nose in a passable imitation of Bodie's habitual movement, Doyle told his partner: 'You could always try walking upwind.'

Bodie finished his drink and put the glass down. He'd hit his own pad and take the bath; but he wasn't going to miss a gibe at good old Ray Doyle.

'Thanks for the hospitality. See you later.'

Bodie let himself out as Doyle started to strip off the combat gear. At that, it was somewhat high . . .

As Bodie got into his car and drove off the dark Porsche eased into view from the opposite direction and moved gently up to Doyle's flat. It remained there for a time, quiescent, like a wild animal patiently waiting at a water hole. Then it as gently moved off and turned into the end street, to continue the observation, unseen.

The Music Hall pub was crowded and filled with laughter and noise and the clink of glasses. Nowhere near as much smoke fouled the atmosphere as there would have been even a few years ago. On the stage a girl – brassy and busty and attired in top hat and tails but still attractive for all that – sang an old time song: 'I'm following in father's footsteps' and her attack was good enough to bring a large part of the audience along with her in the chorus. Maybe they'd all happy memories of a dear old dad.

At one of the tables, wedged in between a party of Northerners out to lap up the sights of the big sinful city, and a group of businessmen who wanted to relax but kept talking about business, Doyle sat talking to Kathie. Bodie was trying to do the same for Jo, the young, rather debby girl, who kept giggling and throwing her arms about in a devastating fashion. Bodie was sincerely concerned for the state of Jo's health.

He indicated the singer who brazened her words out over the stage speakers above the rumbling chorus from the paying customers. 'Good, isn't she?'

Jo giggled and nearly removed Bodie's glass. He rescued it and persevered. 'Good – the singer – the song – good.'

Doyle and Kathie were joining in the song and, at the

same time, taking amusement out of Bodie's predicament. They were going to be of no use to him. The racket in the pub was conducive to singing and drinking, and Bodie glanced at the bar, which was as usual crowded. Jo's fair head fell forward on to the table, trailing a giggle. Her eyes closed.

Bodie stood up. The song was finishing now, a patter of applause scattering like pigeons in Trafalgar Square.

Looking down on Doyle and Kathie, Bodie said with some scathing fierceness: 'I'll leave you two to share memories . . .'

Doyle nodded towards Jo. 'And bring her back some cold water.'

Bodie, suddenly lighter in mood, said: 'Dunk her head in it, more like.'

He wedged his way along between the chairs, apologising every metre of the distance, strained his expensive jacket past a sweaty back, popped out of one crush of the chairs and tables into the new crush at the bar. It would take time to work his way through. Life was a tease at times. Then he saw the singer, minus top hat, trying to get through to the bar.

Bodie smiled.

'Let me get you one –'

To his unastonished pleasure, the singer smiled in return.

At the table, now that Bodie was gone, Doyle could open up a little. He half-lifted his glass in a sketch of a toast. 'Here's to your second interview.'

Kathie made a deprecating gesture. 'If I get one.'

'I'll put in a good word.' Doyle stopped speaking, lowering the glass and half-frowning. 'Maybe I won't. Cowley doesn't like his people getting too involved with each other.'

'We never were.'

Another artiste had mounted the boards and was now warbling on about her old man and following the van, and Doyle leaned a little forward, for the verse was loud but the chorus, when it came, would be thunderous.

'But we – could have been.'

Kathie shook her head. Her eyes were not sad; but their depths revealed an emotion that remained hidden away. 'I was otherwise engaged . . .'

'And now?'

If Kathie read more than Doyle meant her to into his question, she did not reveal that. Their conversation was kept on a light although personal level.

'Unexpectedly available.' She kept it light, not putting off Doyle's gentle approach. 'Unexpectedly available for weddings and barmitzvahs. I thought Cowley doesn't like his operatives getting too close?'

'You're not on the squad yet.'

The hesitation before Kathie spoke was lost on Doyle – for the moment.

'No,' she said, on a breath.

Doyle smiled. 'Still gives us a few days.'

'Yes.'

'But,' said Ray Doyle, at last moving in. 'It doesn't leave us much time.'

'No,' said Kathie.

At that precise moment, as though the atmosphere had percolated into her pretty empty head, Jo sat up and picked up her glass, prepared to carry on talking as though nothing had interrupted what trains of thought were in her mental sidings. She smiled, the glass toppled, Doyle snatched it just in time, and Jo folded forward again, out to the world.

That decided the matter.

Still smiling, Doyle said: 'Shall we?'

Kathie nodded. They both rose, pushing their chairs back and then easing along the crowded floor towards the bar.

Bodie was getting on famously with the singer, whose brassiness was well outweighed by her bustiness. 'Do you have to do another number?'

'Yes. I must go and change . . .'

Bodie, smiling that famous smile, saw Doyle and Kathie squeezing along through the press towards him.

'You two disappearing?' There was no discernible reproof in Bodie's words.

Nodding, Doyle indicated the slumbering Jo, fair head plastered to the table top. 'I think she wants to go home to bed.'

'I should be so lucky.'

Smiling now at his partner's fortune – or misfortune – Doyle attempted an act of gallantry. To the singer, straightfaced, forcing down his smile, he said: 'His sister. Don't let him kid you otherwise.'

Doyle and Kathie went off, smiling more at each other than Bodie and his antics. Bodie attempted a masterly rearguard action. 'Tell me – do you perform every night?'

The St Katherine Docks area was now almost as respectable as any tourist trap in London. Lights festooned and glittered in the water. The tourists were there, too. Doyle and Kathie wandered along, enjoying the luminous evening, looking at the Old Light Ship, just walking and relaxing and enjoying themselves.

Through a more isolated area between warehouses Doyle paused.

'Policemen used to walk here in pairs. Otherwise they were afraid they'd get done up.' They resumed their walk, easily, reflectively. 'This used to be my patch.'

'I know,' said Kathie. 'Maurice Richards used to be your D.S.'

'Maurice keeps a pub down here now.'

'I know. He left the Force.'

'You know a lot?' The rising inflexion in Doyle's voice was not lost on Kathie.

She smiled, and speaking warmly, said: 'Wouldn't you, if you wanted to get into CI5?'

Doyle pondered this. Then he smiled.

'Yeah. Yeah, of course.'

Walking along companionably they made their way back to Doyle's car. As Doyle handed her in and went around to his side of the car, the Porsche lurked half-way around a corner, the driver intently observing all that went on.

When Doyle drove off the Porsche driver waited a moment. Then his headlights flared, a sudden stark brilliance of light in the half-darkness. The Porsche eased out and fell in to the rear of Doyle's car.

'Where are we going?' Kathie wanted to know.

'I thought you'd know.'

Doyle smiled, tooling the car around the corner, heading into the car park of a riverside pub, one of London's joys. Lights glittered on the water, reminding him of the caper when they'd been called to the Festival Hall. They'd wrapped that one up, and the new 180 smg had not proved a long lay off. Heyho . . . There'd be another case for them, soon . . .

Chapter Six

The Jolly Taverner boasted a massive picture window overlooking the Thames from which one obtained a splendid view of the city's watery lifeline and its traffic. Now the last lights flickered across the water, and a gentle breeze stirred tiny wavelets against the tide. Dark bulks of moored lighters cut strangely shaped shadows into that luminescent background.

The pub was comfortable, filled with the curious handiwork of sailors long since gone to Davy Jones. The food was good when it was served during the day; now the serious drinkers were in occupation.

Doyle was very aware of Kathie's arm slipped through his as they came in through the door. He headed straight for the bar where Maurice Richards was in the act of pulling a pint for a customer who in other days Maurice would have pulled in, on the spot, for suspicious behaviour, D&D. Maurice was a burly man with a new and ferocious fuzz of whiskers. His battered face held much wisdom of the evil of the world, and he looked forward to a graceful life pulling pints and pouring shorts, and watching the world and his wife go by.

He did not look up as Doyle fronted the bar, keeping his eye on the level of the bitter and the way the froth spilled, nice and cool over the lip of the glass. 'Won't keep you a minute,' he said, with his practised landlord's charm. The beer pump handle went back with a click and he looked up. His smile changed from the ready-made publican's article to the genuine smile of friendship. 'Ray!'

'Hello, Maurice.'

Maurice plunked the beautifully-drawn pint of bitter down before the anxious customer and swept up the exact money before turning back to Doyle. He beamed.

'Nice to see you again, mate. How're you keeping?'

'Fine, fine. You remember Kathie Mason? C 11?'

Maurice thought for only a moment. 'Yes. Yes, of course I do. Kathie Mason. How are you, Kathie? Still at the Yard?'

' 'Fraid so.'

'What are you now? Inspector?'

There was a snap, perhaps a hidden snap, but, all the same, a definite snap, to Kathie's reply. 'Sergeant.'

Maurice beamed on, ignoring what he suspected. 'Well, keep plugging away. Keeps you young and healthy. Well, well, it is good to see you, mate. What'll you have?'

Insisting the drinks were on the house, Maurice Richards managed to carry on an interesting conversation whilst he served his customers. The evening died out, a stickler for the old rules and regulations, Maurice called time on the dot. The car park emptied, and the drivers were well enough aware of the facts of life to be non-drinkers, at least for the evening. Maurice lowered the lights until only the bar lights were left on. Still talking about the old days, he saw Doyle and Kathie to the door. For a few moments longer they talked and then as Maurice went back inside the Jolly Taverner, Doyle and Kathie got into the car and drove away. Doyle drove carefully. When you met a man like Maurice Richards you suddenly realised what being a copper was about, the routine, the stickling detail, the dedication. Running a pub was a marvellous job, anyone would own that; but, all the same, Maurice was always eager to talk about the old days, when he'd been on the Force . . .

Maurice switched the last lights off over the bar and then crossed to the window over the car park and drew back the curtains. He gave a lost good night look out on to the world.

A dark car was just drawing away, out of the car park, and Maurice gave it a quick look. He frowned. Then, feeling tired, he grimaced and turned away. Bed seemed to him a very interesting prospect . . .

The euphoria in him blended nicely with the sense of expectancy as Ray Doyle climbed the stairway of the block of flats in which Kathie rented a modest apartment. At least, he fancied it would be a modest apartment. As they climbed the stairs, Kathie said: 'You could have used the lift.'

'I like to know who my neighbours are going to be.'

Doyle stopped by a doorway and squinted at the nameplate.

'Sir,' he read. 'Mm – posh. How come – rich daddy?'

Kathie moved to her own door, key in hand, and turned to regard Doyle. She smiled with a fetching warmth.

'Rich boyfriend.'

Doyle took her key with the grand Hollywood gesture.

'Ex – ' he said. He spoke with a shivery premonitory feeling he recognised. Kathie was a grown woman, attractive, desirable, warm. It would be foolish to imagine for a single instant that she had had no experience of life, no affairs, had lived the secluded existence of a nun. But, for this night, at least, this rich boyfriend must take a back seat and very firmly become 'ex'.

He opened the door and stood aside for her. With the slightest catch in her voice Kathie said: 'You know – Cowley's going to put a stop to all this.'

Doyle leaned across and kissed her. It was a light kiss, a preliminary, and it left them both tingling.

'When are you seeing him again?'

'Tomorrow.'

'Well,' said Ray Doyle, and he breathed in and smiled. 'We've got 'till then – haven't we?'

She took back the key and her fingers brushed his. They were trembling. For an instant she paused, searching his face.

'Yes . . . ' said Kathie, and went into her flat, leaving Doyle to follow.

The enigmatic and brooding shape of the Porsche was silhouetted against the street lights. It stood, silent, waiting, outside the block of flats in which Kathie occupied her apartment. When Doyle left very early the following morning, tieless and with his jacket slung over his shoulder, Kathie looked down on him from her window, smiling.

Doyle walked along the pavement past the line of parked cars to reach his own vehicle. A red dot moved with him. It jumped from car window to car window, reflected like a dot of fire, giving a stroboscopic effect. Doyle moved on happily.

Crossing the road to reach his car he checked up and down for traffic and crossed an empty road. The red spot burned in the window of a parked car and then shifted back, along the pavement, going the other way. The red spot halted by the apartment block. Slowly it climbed the wall, past the closed windows.

Like some monstrous legless spider the red spot flared on Kathie's window. It shone into her face.

Still smiling, Kathie blinked, dazzled. She was unaware of what had caused that sudden brilliance of red light, and she turned away and vanished in the shadows of her room.

Doyle slammed his car door, started up and tooled out, still smiling, feeling good. He switched on the car radio and pop music crashed out, complementing his mood.

He headed around the second corner and the car snaked.

Doyle frowned.

His driving couldn't be that bad . . .

The road pitched sharply downhill towards a busy junction.

The wheel felt slack, like chewed gum, under his hands. Doyle abruptly realised what was on.

Wrestling with the wheel he stamped on the brakes.

The car howled on. Again and again Doyle lashed the brakes, hauling on the handbrake; the car did not slacken speed. The speedo jerked around, mounting, pelting up through the numbers as the car sped down the hill.

The grimness in Ray Doyle's face, the flashing houses

going past, the hammering on the brakes, the wheel twisting this way and that . . . Helplessly, Ray Doyle was carried whirling down the hill.

The old houses on the corner had been pulled down and already this early in the morning the men were at work, tractors and dumpers chugging, cranes lifting loads, men in orange jackets and helmets shouting, the ripe smell of dust and ancient dirt hanging in the air.

Doyle's car howled down the hill.

The junction was whirring up to him with cars and buses passing in a steady stream with the lights. He snaked around a car, the wheel giving him just enough control. He saw the demolition site. His fierce look clamped down.

With a savage and final twist to the wheel he got the car off its line of headlong disaster. The crash as the car hit the pavement jolted him up in the seat. The car swerved. Headlong it went through the wooden fencing around the demolition site. It ploughed over and through a pile of timber. Dust and wooden chips spouted. On the car surged, wobbling, shaking, jerking over a couple of wheelbarrows.

Orange-clad men were yelling. A crane driver leaned over and hoicked his load out of the way just in time.

Away from the deadly junction Doyle managed to twist the car, full into and through the demolition site. The car roared on, plunging into a pile of yellow sand. Like a road grader the car scraped the sand up in a golden fountain.

With a shuddering moaning crash the car stopped, juddering.

Doyle sat behind the wheel. He did not shake – but he was shaken up, no doubt of that.

Ray Doyle was a professional.

His instincts of self-preservation were working at full stretch. This wasn't the end of it . . . There was further danger . . .

For a scarlet instant of horror he thought the door was jammed and wouldn't open. He bashed it with his heel, kicking with bent leg. The door snapped open.

With a gasp Ray Doyle tumbled out, rolling, lifting up

and running a few paces before he hurled himself over the shifting mound of yellow sand. Sand clogged into his face and eyes and hair, jammed up his nostrils. But his ears caught the smashing impact of the explosion. The whole world turned orange. The blast caromed over him, lashing his shirt. Bits and pieces of his car rained down.

Cautiously, Doyle put an eye over the heap of sand. Black smoke rose from tangled wreckage.

Quite a way to start the day . . .

Bodie's lips wrinkled as he leaned across and opened the door for Doyle. Doyle looked a mess. An ambulance stood by and the police were fussing with the blown-up wreck. The orange garbed construction workers gawped.

'Can't leave you on your own for a minute, can I?'

Doyle swallowed down, hard. He felt outraged. He got in and sat down, squarely, glowering on the morning.

'Somebody tried to kill me.'

'I had figured that out.'

'But who?'

Bodie took his car out gently and turned down towards the junction that was now merely a crossroads and no longer a disaster area. 'Don't you know?'

'No.'

'You've got that many enemies?'

Doyle breathed in through pinched nostrils. He could still feel the car under him, snaking uselessly, the wheel idle in his fists, the brakes like a tub of treacle.

'I mean – if we were on a case . . . '

'But we're not.'

'So,' said Doyle, bitterly. 'Why?'

'Jealous lover?' said Bodie. He perked up. 'Husband?'

'Married birds are not my scene.'

'I see. Get on all right last night, did you?'

Doyle made no reply. He sat hunched, glowering, his round face and curly hair pugnacious.

Bodie sighed. 'Don't ask me how I got on, will you?'

'All right,' said Doyle, rousing himself. 'How did you get on last night?'

'Don't ask,' said Boyle.

When they reached Doyle's flat Bodie decided it was time he recovered a little of his lost fun-and-games. Ever since they'd been given the assignment of checking out the 180 smg he'd had the strongest conviction that he'd been on the sticky end. Oh, not in the big way that Ray Doyle had just been; there had been no attempt to sabotage his car and blow him up. But, all the same, as he checked Doyle at the door and produced his Browning auto, he fancied that what he was doing wasn't all play-acting.

'A-ah,' he said, as the door opened and he looked warily in.

'What?' said Doyle with visions of a shower obsessing him.

'Watch it, son.'

So, only half-joking, Bodie went in. He went into the drilled routine they knew as 'entering a dangerous place where there is a gunman hiding'. He did it for real. Despite all the jokes, you never knew . . .

He checked the entrance over and then beckoned Doyle to follow. He played it up. Not really appreciating Bodie's clowning, Doyle went in as his partner threw open the living room door. All the same . . . Ray Doyle drew his own gun as they went through. Just in case . . .

Side by side they stood looking over the room.

It looked clean.

But you could never really tell . . .

Crossing the room, Bodie checked the drapes, looked through into the kitchen, came back. He was standing near the wall cupboard. He put his left hand on the cupboard door, ready to move off, and the door eased open a fraction.

Bodie pivoted. His eyebrows drew down.

'Doyle!'

Doyle crossed to the cupboard as though on skates. Together they stood looking at the fractionally-opened door, fearing the worst. With great care Bodie eased the cupboard door open.

The 180 smg and the bag of ammunition were no longer there.

'Cowley's going to love this,' said Doyle.

His partner looked at him.

'You're in trouble, mate. Big trouble.'

That was no understatement.

Reporting in at CI5 headquarters, a run-down and undistinguished building off Whitehall, the partners went down with George Cowley to the subterranean garage with attached workshops. The whole building was scruffy and ill-used, only the forensic, communications and garage areas being spick-and-span and crammed with the most modern equipment. Essentials were what mattered with Cowley. Now an essential had been stolen – stolen from his own men – and he did not like it. He did not like it one little bit. He was steaming with fury as they went through into the garage.

Again, he pointed out the obvious: 'The gun was in your care, Doyle.'

'Yes, sir.'

'So – where is it?'

'I don't know.'

'No.' Cowley led the way out on to the concrete apron. 'Somebody does.'

'But,' said Doyle, helplessly. 'Who? How?'

'Find out, Doyle.' Cowley's face held that grim, lined, bull-dog look that would put the frights up the biggest villains in any racket. 'Find out. Fast.'

Quietly, Bodie pointed out: 'The suppliers knew we had it.'

'They didn't know you were testing it. But somebody did. And somebody knew where to find your car last night.'

'The two things can't be connected,' protested Doyle.

'Must be.' Bodie spoke with brisk conviction. 'Too much of a coincidence.'

'Then what are you standing around here for?' Cowley turned on them, making them brace up. 'Get out and connect them! Before I have the pair of you drummed out of

CI5 for incompetence. Can you think of any good reason why I shouldn't?'

Cowley strode over to where his white Rover 3500 was parked under the strip lights, facing the exit ramp. He half-halted to listen to Doyle.

'Yes, sir. You want that gun back and you think we're the best operatives to do it.'

Cowley's head ducked down as he prepared to enter the car. The partners didn't know if the movement was merely that of the chief getting his head down to avoid bashing it on the roof, or a gesture of acceptance of Doyle's reasoning. Ruth sat behind the steering wheel, prim, proper, and keeping herself well-removed from the fracas going on.

From inside the car, leaning forward and looking up, Cowley made it crystal clear.

'Right! I want that gun back! I don't care what you have to do to get it – and if you could avoid getting yourselves killed, I'd be grateful. Replacements are expensive.'

Ruth started the car.

Doyle stepped back. 'It hurts, too!'

Cowley waved Ruth on and the Rover trundled out and up the exit ramp. A puff of blue exhaust smoke hung for a moment, smelling, and then dissipated in the ventilation.

Doyle and Bodie were left on the concrete, the noise of the car fading, to stare at each other and sigh.

Chapter Seven

The forensic experts and the garage techs checked over what was left of Doyle's car. They checked painstakingly and very thoroughly. What they had to say made Doyle look even more sick, and drew Bodie's eyebrows down in that ferocious frown of his.

'He did four separate operations,' Jack, the chief tech told them. 'So why did he go to so much trouble?'

'Four?' Bodie looked up from the mangled hulk.

The garage looked functional with the cars gleaming under the overhead strip lighting, the white-coated techs moving about, the flicker of needles around dials and the low-humming vibrations of motors.

'One,' said Jack, ticking them off on his fingers. 'He loosened the wheel nuts. Two, he fixed the brakes, very carefully, so they'd fail after they'd been applied once or twice. Not right away.'

'Three,' cut in Doyle. 'Steering?'

Jack touched his third finger. 'Loosened nuts again.'

'Four?' said Bodie.

'I'd have thought number four was obvious even to you, Bodie. Four, he stuck an explosive device under the engine. And that's what makes it really funny.'

'Why didn't the bomb go off 'til after I'd crashed?'

'That's it.' Jack had seen it all. He knew a thousand and one ways of rigging a car into a murder weapon. But there was the safe old standard way. 'If you wanted to kill somebody with a car bomb, what would you do?'

Doyle's mouth drew down. 'Wire it to the ignition.' His finger and thumb lifted and twisted in the air, as though he turned an ignition key. Then he abruptly threw both hands upwards, splayed, in a gruesome mime of an explosion.

'Right. So why all this monkey business with brakes and steering? And why a device with an impact fuse – designed to go off about thirty seconds after a crash?'

'Long enough to give me time to get out.'

'Maybe,' said Bodie. 'Maybe he wasn't trying to kill you. Some sort of joker?'

'Some joke.' Doyle sounded grim. 'Thanks, Jack.'

The daylight outside in the garage yard, tucked in under the grimy walls, made them blink after the flourescents. Bodie's car – the one he'd drawn from the pool for his own use this week, a black Jaguar 420, eleven years old but in perfect mechanical condition and just right for any undercover job – waited. Both CI5 operatives walked across and started to open the doors. Then they paused. They looked at each other.

As one they bent down and looked under the car.

When they were satisfied that what they saw was Jaguar and not bomb, they straightened up. There was no need to smile even a little apologetically at each other. Being a professional, an agent of the Big A, meant you did what you had to do to stay alive.

Bodie did say: 'Never know, do you?'

They drove off back to Doyle's flat, and the thoughts of each man were not the kind of thoughts a Sunday School teacher would wish communicated to her class.

Forensic experts from CI5 were just clearing their gear away as the partners arrived. Nothing had been found. Whoever had lifted the 180 knew what he was doing. Clues – they were like icebergs up the Congo.

'How did, whoever it was, know the gun was here?' demanded Bodie as they prepared the essential cup of tea.

'Somebody told 'em?'

'Who knew?'

'You and me,' said Doyle. 'Cowley. Ruth –'

Bodie said: 'Kathie?'

'No.' Doyle was positive. 'For all she knew I'd taken it back to the armoury.'

'Wish you had.'

'That car – ' Doyle lowered his cup. 'The day we got the 180 – you remember – that chase up the dual – '

'Yeah. You reckon – ?'

'I don't know.'

'Start at the beginning.' Bodie screwed his eyes up. He became absorbed. 'Who'd want that gun? And why?'

'Gangs. Terrorists.'

'Not unless the gangs had some executions lined up. Even so, they'd be better off with shotguns. And terrorists do well enough with ordinary gear.'

'For long-distance assassination? The 180 is heap big medicine. Pay up – or else. Do it our way, or else. The red dot's enough for that kind of message.'

'So it could have been nicked for money.'

'If that is it – if it is – they'd have to sell it, wouldn't they?'

'Right.'

'So,' said Bodie, standing up and putting his tea cup back into the saucer with accuracy. 'To quote Cowley – what are we sitting around for?'

'What indeed?' said Doyle as both men made for the door.

The Woolwich Free Ferry might have lost a deal of the grandeur the cross-river service once possessed; it remained a remarkable achievement considering the age; the age of the service and the age in which it now found itself. The ferries chugged out in their neat figure-of-eights, churning the water into a green, foam-tinged maelstrom, chungling along, in and out, across and back, over and over. The sights and smells of the river were translated into the sights and smells of the open ocean, where clippers raced under towering piles of canvas, beating around the Horn – to those small boys who dreamed the day away, travelling back and forth, back and forth.

And there was always the young lady who stowed away

and bestowed her seductive favours on the deckhand not to give her away on the passage to New York . . .

Across and back, across and back . . .

Bodie spotted Martell on the upper deck. Martell had all the attributes of the successful city businessman – he would not thank you for calling him a city gent – from the dark hat, the dark suit and the dark look about the eyes. He radiated the solidarity of gilt-edged stock. He wore a dark red carnation. He looked prosperous, and if there was the slightest twitch in the corner of his eyes, in the elegantly pig-skinned hands, that would be put down to a post-prandial brandy too much. Erroneously put down, as Bodie knew only too well.

Shaking hands, Bodie said: 'Marty.' He put warmth into the greeting. The summons had been swift and swiftly answered.

'Bodie, dear chap. Good to see you again.'

Taking in the deck of the ferry, the sway and surge of her as she plugged across the river, the passengers, the iron railings, the companionways, Bodie said: 'I like your new offices.'

'You know me, Bodie. Always feel – restricted – in four walls.' He stared shrewdly at Doyle, who returned the stare. 'Walls have ears.'

'Marty – Ray Doyle. We're partners. Marty Martell.'

Martell left off scrutinising Doyle and gestured down river. 'Beautiful, isn't it? Amazing to think, a few hundred years ago the Vikings used to sail up here – raid our cities – '

'Rob all the women,' said Doyle. 'And rape the men.'

'Martell's one of the world's experts,' said Bodie.

'I specialise in handguns and rifles.'

'Sporting?' said Doyle. 'Hunting rifles?'

'If that's what you want, yes.'

'And,' said Doyle, his voice softening and thereby becoming incredibly conspiratorial. 'If I want something else?'

'I think,' said Marty Martell with a quick look about

him. 'I really do think, my dear chap, we'd better go into my other office.'

So they clattered down the companionway on to another deck where some of the twitch evaporated from the arms dealer.

'You remember that consignment of Uzis you wanted for the Gulf, that time, Bodie? Remember the job we had getting them out there? And getting the money out of the ruler? I hope this isn't that sort of deal, Bodie. What do you want?'

'No deal, not this time, Marty. We want your help. What do you know about the American 180 smg?'

'You want 180s?' Martell screwed his face up, which gave him a dyspeptic look. 'That's difficult. Distribution is very tightly controlled.' He shook his head. 'That's a real meanie, you know.'

'We know. We've tried one,' Doyle told him.

'There's one loose in London, right now,' said Bodie.

'No.'

'True.'

'That's bad.' Martell's face betrayed the way he was quickly evaluating the worth of this information. 'That's very bad.'

'You haven't heard anything?'

'Not a whisper. I don't think it can be on the market.'

The partners explained to Marty just how the 180 had been hijacked and the arms dealer looked more unhappy the more he heard. He did not even take a rise out of the professionals.

'A 180 loose in London is bad news. Very bad for the business. Not good for our reputation.'

'It doesn't do much for ours, either.'

'All right,' said Martell. 'Leave it with me. I'll ask around.'

When Marty Martell, after shaking hands, left them the partners leaned on the rail and watched the approaching shore coming up, with, as always, the impression that the ferry was going right on up into the clutter of buildings and heading for the North Circular on her own steam.

'Now what?'

Doyle spoke a little uncertainly. 'Start at the other end.'

'Any end in particular?'

'Look up a few old friends.'

They stepped off the ferry and headed for their car parked a little ways off. Bodie was in front fishing for the Jag's keys. A red dot suddenly appeared, springing into life on Doyle's back.

Bodie opened his door and reaching across unlocked the passenger side door. Doyle leaned down, opened the door and the red dot stayed with him. A splotch of red light on his back, hard, ugly, infinitely menacing, the red dot zeroed him into the sights.

Ducking down to enter the Jag, Doyle moved.

The wing mirror exploded into flying shards of glass.

The crack of the shot sent the partners diving to the ground by the car. As they hit their Brownings appeared in their fists. They peered out, eyes scouring the car park and the surrounding buildings.

'Your life – or mine?' demanded Bodie.

Very grimly, Doyle spat out: 'Mine!'

He hesitated. Then, moving slowly, he stood up. He exposed himself to the sniper. For a long pause nothing happened. Then Bodie rose and joined his partner.

Bodie looked about, his mouth firmed, his eyebrows dinting down. 'I think he's playing with us.' He sounded disgusted. 'Cat and mouse. Stringing us along. And he knows all the moves.'

'Well,' said Doyle. 'Most of them. Let's get out of here. I feel a bit exposed.'

When the black Jaguar had tooled out of the car park the 180 was withdrawn into the window of the Porsche. The dark foreign car waited, and then, gently, rolled away after the Jaguar.

Doyle's next port of call was the yacht and powerboat marina along the river and here he led Bodie along the serried ranks of boats to Brownie's large and functional cabin cruiser.

'Gets about a bit, does Brownie.'

'Just let him get about a bit and come up with a sniff on the 180.'

But Brownie hadn't heard a sneeze. He had worked for Doyle before, on a strictly favour-for-favour basis, and offered to do a little sniffing. When they went back along the catwalk Doyle marched with a swing, out in the open. Bodie hurried after him. The moment Bodie caught up, Doyle slowed down and began sauntering along the tow-path.

'I always knew it,' said Bodie. 'You're as mad as he is.'

'Who?'

'The nutter! Ambling about. He could be anywhere within a thousand yards – right now! – and take a pot shot. He couldn't miss you.'

'That's right. But he won't.' Doyle was now firmly of the opinion that he was right and had summed up what was going on. 'Not yet. He's teasing me. He's not just a nutter, he's a sadistic nutter. And he's setting me up.'

'For something nasty. And you're going to – ?'

' 'til he comes out of cover to get me.'

'And then?' Bodie eyed his partner with deep concern.

'Why, then, Bodie, you'll be around to save me. I hope.'

A radio call came in the moment they were back in the car and Doyle found a phone box and called Maurice Richards who urgently wanted to talk with him.

In the Jolly Taverner Maurice answered the phone and at once became alert when Doyle got through.

'Ray – I've been trying to reach you.'

'What is it?'

'Couple of things. I couldn't swear to it; but when you left here last night I thought I saw a car follow you.

'What sort?'

'Porsche. Didn't get the number, too dark.'

'Thanks – you said a couple of things?'

Maurice leaned back on the bar. A glint of light speared up from the bottle array. He squinted his eyes, puzzled. A dot of red light suddenly shone clear on the big bottle of

Bell's. Curious, he took the phone across to the picture window overlooking the river.

'I couldn't say anything much last night . . . ' Maurice paused. Then, in a strange puzzled voice: 'What the – ?'

The red dot of light shone through the clear window and settled on his forehead.

'Maurice?' said Doyle over the phone.

The big picture window exploded. Maurice Richards was flung back, his head exploding backwards, the phone crashing up and over to hit the floor with a smash. Maurice toppled, his eyes wide and horrified. There was not much of the top of his head left.

'Maurice!' yelled Doyle. '*Maurice!*'

The investigations into the death of Maurice Richards went through routinely; but George Cowley went down to the Jolly Taverner, and he was harshly determined to go a damn sight past routine to get to the bottom of this. The point two two that had killed Maurice Richards had been fired from a 180 smg. So that meant Richards had something to do with it all – or did it?

Cowley wanted to know what Richards had told Doyle.

'The car tailing me – as for the other thing – that's splattered all over the wall with his brains. Poor Maurice . . . '

Bodie said: 'Next stop – poor you.'

'But it must have been something he already knew, because he got as far as saying it was something he hadn't been able to tell me last night.'

'So at last,' said Cowley with some force. 'We have some related facts. He's after Richards and Doyle and not you, Bodie. Rigging the car bomb could've been a grudge against CI5. Taking the 180? Possible also. But killing an ex-cop? Stalking you? You're Richards's ex-bully boy. Ex-cop.'

'So it's nothing to do with CI5,' ventured Bodie.

'This is something out of your past, Doyle.' Cowley looked at the big shattered window. 'Out of your time at the Yard. Someone who hates you so much he wants to see you squirm before he brings you to your knees –'

'And then,' said Bodie with gruesome cheerfulness. 'Puts a bullet through your head.' He smiled warmly. 'We ought to check through your friends.'

'Exactly,' said Cowley. 'And those inside first. I have the police and prison service checking their records.'

Doyle could not bring at once to mind any hard-cases he and Maurice Richards had put away in their time together he anticipated would go to these lengths, so Cowley arranged for him to check the records. This was an office chore, and Doyle made a face; but it was his life on the line.

Because of the involvement already in hand with CI5 Kathie was seconded on direct orders of the Commissioner to help out. She brought the files in great armloads, and Doyle worked his way through them in the sleazy old office put at his disposal.

'You were a busy young copper, weren't you. The terror of Stepney Green.'

'Was. You're sure about tonight?'

'Quite. Where will you be?'

'At home, going through these – if you get hungry.'

Kathie leaned over and kissed the top of his head. 'Good. We don't want you wandering around the streets, do we?'

'Not without Bodie to look after me . . .'

'Or me.' Kathie touched her fingers to her lips and then pressed them against his. 'Ciao.'

Doyle sighed as she went out and returned to the files. He bent over them fiercely, muttering to himself. 'C'mon, you nutter. Talk to me, talk to me . . .'

The rest of the day passed. Bodie contacted Martell who reported he had a nibble for a buyer for the 180 but nothing else. Cowley spent the day and the night sifting grimly through files, aided by Ruth who spiked his coffee with brandy. Doyle took his files home and went through them, throwing them aside, one by one, discovering exactly nothing of any spectre from his past who wished sadistically to torture him and then kill him. Correction – there were plenty of those; but not one currently legally or illegally on the outside.

Parked outside Doyle's flat, Bodie passed an uncomfortable night, not by any means the first in his adventurous life. But he was totally unaware of the red spot which fastened lovingly on his car, and then the back of his head – and passed on.

When, with the milkman and the sparrows, dawn trundled around Bodie stretched and yawned and attempted to put his spine back where his backbone ought to be. Doyle opened the blinds and looked out and saw his partner's car, and smiled, and went on back to put the kettle on. Moments later the doorbell rang.

'Good morning,' said Bodie's voice. 'This is your friendly night watchman. How about some breakfast?'

Doyle spoke into the flat intercom. 'Come on up.' He pressed the button to release the outside door to the block.

Bodie rolled in, yawning, matching Doyle's yawn. The kettle started to sing and Doyle shuffled off to make tea.

'Couldn't you find anywhere better to sleep?'

'Who's been sleeping?' demanded Bodie, aggrieved. 'Anyway, I've kipped down in worse places. In Africa – '

'Where?'

'Never mind. Where's my breakfast?' He licked his lips. 'Bacon, egg, tomatoes, sausage, fried bread, baked beans. What've you got?'

Doyle smiled smugly. 'A spot of natural yoghurt and a couple of slices of stale wholemeal. Be all right toasted.'

'Aah! I'm starving, Doyle.'

The doorbell rang again and this time it was Kathie. She came in, smiling. 'Are you all right?'

'Like you see,' said Doyle, returning the big smile.

'Great. What's burning, then?'

Bodie yelped. 'The toast!'

By the time Bodie had rescued the curled black cinder from under the grill and deposited it in the waste bin, Kathie opened her basket, telling them she'd brought in breakfast supplies. 'And I met your postman as I was coming in. Here.' She handed across a couple of nasty official-looking letters and a book-sized parcel. 'Feels like a book. In a plain wrapper? What are you buying . . . ?' Her voice tailed away at the expressions on the men's faces.

'Doyle . . . '

'Yeah . . . Kathie, love, put it down, very gently on the table and walk away.'

'Oh my God!' Kathie put the package on the table. 'You don't think . . . ?'

They sent Kathie out, and she went, reluctantly, trembling.

From the drawer Doyle took out a small tool kit and scissors and gently, gingerly, with a concentration that brought the watching Bodie's breath hard through his pinched nostrils, he cut the string and began cutting carefully into the wrapping. A wire was exposed. The scissors snipped around carefully. The tension screwed in, fierce and bringing sweat to their foreheads.

A red dot appeared on the ceiling. It wandered across the wall, zig-zagged, came back, travelled across the table towards the package with that glinting exposed wire.

'Doyle . . . '

'Go!' shouted Doyle.

The partners dived headlong out of the way and through the open bedroom door. The window erupted in a smash of breaking glass and the package whipped off the table as though hooked up by a skeleton fishing hook. Bodie and Doyle crouched, hands over the backs of their necks, head down, waiting for the explosion – that did not come.

Presently they whooshed in deep breaths, stood up and went back to the room. Doyle picked up the package, snipped through the wire and ripped the paper away. He looked at the book inside.

Moriarty's Police Law.

'Your friend,' said Kathie, appearing in the doorway. 'Has a sense of humour.'

Chapter Eight

If Jack had been contemptuous of the attempts on Doyle's car he was positively scathing about the so-called book-bomb.

'He's making fools of us,' said Doyle. The garage hummed and rang with activity, and the partners glowered down at the spread remains of the so-called bomb. 'This was never meant to go off. It was wired wrong. What's he playing at?'

Cowley appraised Doyle coolly. 'You don't know? Another taunt, another turn of the screw. Don't you know your man yet? Doesn't this tell you?' He tapped the book. 'Doesn't it, Doyle?'

Doyle made a little helpless gesture. 'I've been through every file – '

'And the man we want is in half of them. Names, Doyle. Names of every man released from Her Majesty's Prisons in the last six months. Including ex-Detective Superintendent Preston and ex-Detective Inspector Montgomery.'

'You know them?' Bodie saw Doyle's look. 'And either of them – '

' – would hate you enough to murder you,' Cowley continued. 'You didn't *work* on their case – you were *part* of it! Police evidence came primarily from yourself – and one other.'

Doyle said: 'Maurice Richards.'

'Well,' snapped Cowley, turning away, already busy. 'Find them, lads. Find them!'

The suburban house looked neat and well-cared-for, as

though the man about the house had plenty of time to spare for gardening and painting jobs. Preston was carrying armloads of weeds across to the compost heap when Bodie's Jaguar screeched up fast and hauled into the kerb. Preston looked up. He was a tough, powerful man in his forties, with short hair and a jaw on which the bristle showed blue. His face tautened and relaxed as Doyle came up the garden path followed by Bodie.

'Mr Preston.'

'Doyle,' said Preston. A muscle jumped alongside his jaw. 'What are we in such a hurry about?'

'We just wanted to see how you were. What you'd been up to since your release.'

Preston carried on with the weeds, limp and dark green, going down the side of the house. 'Are you still on the Force?'

'No. CI5.'

Preston's attitude betrayed nothing, but again that muscle jumped. After a moment he said flatly: 'Yes, that'd suit you, Doyle. Congratulations . . . '

'Have you seen anything of Maurice Richards since you've been out?'

'Only what I read in the papers.' He went on walking and the partners followed. Everything seemed normal; but the atmosphere was there, intangible as smoke; but there. 'I was sorry about that. Not a CI5 job, though, is it?'

Bodie was sizing up the house and Doyle watched Preston dump the small weeds on the compost. He put it directly. 'Where were you yesterday afternoon at 4.15?'

Preston twisted his tough face up. 'That takes me back a bit. I used to say things like that. I was with my probation officer.'

'Where?'

'Miles away from Maurice Richards, if that's what you're thinking. Greenwich. I got stuck down there, as a matter of fact. There was a terrible traffic jam in the Rotherhithe tunnel. A big truck had broken down.'

'You've a car, then, have you?'

They walked back to the garage and Doyle looked in.

The car was a red Mini.

'Where were you the night before?'

'Night before last, you mean.' Preston screwed up his eyes. 'I had a drink down at the local, then I got an early night.'

'With your wife?'

Preston's face turned sour. 'Don't make me laugh. My wife left me five years ago.' As Doyle started to say he was sorry, Preston cut in savagely: 'You don't have to be. It was never much of a marriage.' He looked ostentatiously at his watch. 'Now you'll have to excuse me, if you don't mind. I've an appointment.'

'With your probation officer again?'

Preston's face revealed a sudden fierce flash of anger and contempt. Then he turned away, under control once more. 'It's a condition of parole, 'til I've got a steady job. Which could be a long time. Nobody loves a bent copper – do they?' He halted at the back door and stood, quite evidently blocking the way. His chin lifted. 'You weren't thinking of coming in, were you? Without a warrant?'

With that he turned and went into his house. He made that turn and his exit a contemptuous slap around the face. Bodie's eyebrows drew down. Doyle nodded at his partner and started for the car. After a moment, Bodie followed.

As he started the Jag up, Bodie said: 'You don't exactly love each other, do you?'

'As he said. Nobody loves a bent copper.'

Driving away, Bodie said: 'Let's go and see the other one.'

Ex-Detective Inspector Montgomery did not live quite so well as his ex-chief. But the long block of GLC council flats was clean and the outside balconies were swept. The dustbins were stashed away in a bricked area and most of them had lids. The CI5 men rang the doorbell of Montgomery's flat. The bell rang and rang and nothing else happened until the next door opened and a large and cheerful West Indian woman came out and stood regarding them. She wore an extravagantly-flowered dress and white slippers. The partners rang the bell by turn and the

West Indian lady just stood there, looking at them.

After a bit Bodie flashed her his big smile and said: 'Afternoon.'

'No good you ringing that bell, man.'

'No?'

The lady gestured with her shining arms. 'Mr Montgomery, he gone away.'

Doyle said: 'When? When did he go?'

Bodie said: 'Where?'

The West Indian lady drew herself up. 'I don't know, man. What you think I am? A nosey parker or something? I mind my own damn business. You mind yours.'

The professionals exchanged glances. Then, like chastised schoolboys – although both raging and uproariously hilarious inside – they took themselves off down the concrete stairway.

When Doyle got back to his pad the phone was ringing. He crossed the room with a care to check first that left him stone cold aware of the situation he was in. That sadistic maniac was out to torture and kill him, if CI5 didn't get to him first.

He picked up the phone. It was Brownie whose boat business got him about a bit and who was happy to do Ray Doyle the odd favour. 'Hello, Brownie. You got something for me?'

'I think so. Can we meet?'

'Yes. When? I'll come to the boat –'

'No – in an hour. I'm out East.' Brownie hunched over the phone, tense. 'Tell you what – you know the old depot, by the shunting yards?'

'What are you doing there?'

Brownie's voice husked. 'No questions, Ray.'

'It's a big place, Brownie. I'll meet you half way –'

'No. No, I've got to wait it out. I'll park my motor at the far end of the second roadway. You'll see it.'

Brownie's fist on the receiver gripped his knuckles into yellow skulls.

'Okay,' said Doyle's voice in his ear. 'In an hour. Right. See you.'

Slowly, Brownie lowered the phone. He missed the cradle. He was scared clean through. Hell! What a note – doing a favour for an old mate.

The muzzle of the 180 smg snugged almost under his chin. Holding the weapon in a comfortable grip, Preston gently twitched the barrel up. The cruel muzzle jolted under Brownie's chin, dinting his Adam's Apple. Preston smiled.

In his sailing days Brownie had seen sharks with a warmer grin than that.

Bodie threw the Jaguar into a skidding stop in his usual reckless way and jumped out to ring Doyle's doorbell. He saw there was no car outside; but he rang, anyway. When there was no answer he went back to his car and called HQ. They told him Doyle had called in, said he was going to meet a contact and was maintaining radio silence. Bodie nodded. The bastard who was running rings around them had clearly been listening in on their frequency. So he tooled the car out fast towards the riverside marina. Brownie would be the contact, for sure.

Brownie's efficient cruiser was deserted. Bodie poked around and called: 'Doyle. Brownie,' a couple of times. Nothing. He went forrard, crouching a little to get into the forecastle. The smell of bilges and damp wood hit him. A light from the scuttle showed him a flap-down table beside the rumpled bunk.

On the small table, upright, gleaming brassily, stood a point two two cartridge. Bodie looked for the time it takes for a spider to blink an eye – then he was up and out and along the catwalk as though all the sharks of all the oceans were snapping at his heels.

Cowley was sitting in his car with Ruth driving when he contacted Bodie, and he listened to the latest news with that dangerous set to his jaw that spoke of storms blowing up.

'Listen, Bodie. That missing copper, Montgomery . . .

we've located him. He's been with his family on a fishing holiday in Scotland for the past two weeks. Get around to Preston's house. Fast. I'll meet you there.'

Bodie slammed the radiophone away and tromped on the gas. The big Jaguar howled along, heading for the quiet suburban street trailing a lifting wake of dust.

Time, time... It was all against the men of CI5 now...

Wheels locked, tyres smoking, the Jaguar skidded into the kerb of the pavement before Preston's neat little house. Bodie leaped out, left the door open, hared up the path. He banged on the door, listened, heard no sounds from within, belted around the side passage to the back. The closed, glass-paned back door beckoned. He snatched up the old piece of sacking Preston had been using for his weeds and wrapped it around his fist. His lips were thinned out. He drew his Browning auto. He lifted the sack-covered fist ready to smash it through the glass – the automatic snouted ready for an instant blast.

He swung.

The door opened sharply.

Bodie, on the swing, almost fell through.

Cowley said, unsmiling: 'At last, Bodie. I thought we said – hurry!'

Bodie recovered himself. He breathed in very deeply and an observer might have thought he said a short quick prayer.

'Yes, sir. I had further to come –'

'Well, come in, man, come in. I thought,' said Cowley, leading the way into the house. 'You'd like to know what we found.'

That, fulminated Bodie, was just like George Cowley...

They went through into the kitchen where two CI5 operatives continued to stand their guard, one at the door leading on to the passage. Bodie was surprised to see Kathie there. As he came in she turned away from the wall-cupboard which, although clean, was a good few years old, and gave him a pleasant smile.

'Hi, Kathie,' said Bodie.

The other CI5 man stood off a little to the side. Bodie

knew them both, useful chaps to have around on your side in an argument. Cowley went across to the formica-topped kitchen table and scooped up two coloured scraps of papers, stapled together. He tossed the tickets to Bodie, who caught them almost without looking, as you take a slip catch, whilst his gaze swivelled back to Kathie.

He looked back, away from her, down to the tickets.

'Two airline tickets – for Buenos Aires – who . . . ?'

Even for Bodie it took a moment to sink it.

He looked back to Kathie. She just stood, smiling pleasantly, quite composed.

Cowley said : 'Yes, Bodie. That's what we found. And what Maurice Richards knew. Preston and Miss Mason were married before he went inside. Seven years ago . . .'

Bodie clenched his hands into fists, the airline tickets crumpling. He had to hold himself in. His face drew down, tautly and he could feel the quiver right through him, right from his ankles up past his scalp and crackling in his hair.

'You bitch ! You set Doyle up !'

Cowley watched, ready instantly to step in. Kathie Mason went on smiling her cold smile.

Bodie controlled himself. It was damned hard; but there were things he had to know and things to be done, done damn quick . . .

'She set us up from the start ! He didn't even have to follow us. He knew exactly where Doyle was going to be. Didn't he ?' He flared around at Kathie. 'And you know where he is now. Well ?'

Kathie said nothing. Her look, the smile now congealing with contempt, plainly told Bodie he could go and drop dead. Bodie fancied she wasn't fully aware of the true situation. Cowley nodded to Bodie. Then the chief of CI5 turned mildly away.

Bodie moved nearer to Kathie. He stood, tall, seeming to loom over the girl who had betrayed his partner.

'You'd better tell me, my lovely. Because if anything happens to Doyle, I'll find your sadistic boyfriend –'

'– husband !' interjected Kathie, sharply.

'– and I'll kill him, very, very slowly. And then to save you the pleasure of spending the rest of your life in jail I'll do the same for you. With great joy . . .'

Kathie had been a policewoman a long time. Making sergeant and being passed over for inspector had embittered her, sure; but she knew police procedures. She turned to Cowley, a rising flush in her cheeks, ready to demand her rights. Threats meant nothing. 'Did you hear that, Mr Cowley?'

Speaking with that measured accent, the plum very evident in his mouth, Cowley said: 'I never heard a word, Miss Mason. Not a single word.'

Kathie's face quivered and she flinched back by a fraction.

Bodie amplified. 'His eyesight's not much good, either.'

The railway tracks lined out like strung taffy. Grimy brick sheds rose cutting off the view inland, and the river wallowed along by the tidal-wall, grey and somehow slimy in this particular reach. A deal of container traffic was done here and the container wagons lined out, some fully loaded, some half-loaded and some empty. Just at the moment there was a lull and the yards held that empty, hollow, somehow dusty look of inactivity that envelops man-made business when that business is not being done. Doyle drove in carefully and headed for the rendezvous with Brownie. From cabin cruisers to container-shunting yards was a tall step; but Brownie had sounded – odd.

The container, overhead gantry and racks with dangling chains lifted ahead and Doyle pulled over and stopped the car. He got out. The silence oppressed him, even the thin screeching of distant gulls, fighting over scraps along the waterline, couldn't lift that leaden feeling. The smells of engine oil and grease, of the exotic perfumes of the Orient and last week's cabbages, blended. A red dot appeared on the side of Doyle's car.

Doyle spotted the crawling red spot. It swerved along the side of the car towards him.

Instantly he hurled himself flat, rolled around the

bumper and slid down on the far side. The gun was in his fist, drawn with the same quicksilver reflexes that had hurled him into cover.

The sky lowered greyly; it would rain soon, as it was continuing to rain this wet summer; but Doyle's gaze searched carefully along the cranes and warehouse buildings.

'Where are you?' he bellowed, suddenly.

A voice shrieked up the scale, near cracking. 'Over here, Ray! Ray!'

Doyle spun about. He had scanty cover and he made a run for the gaunt scarecrow of the gantry, sprinting the distance. No bullet pocks kicked dust at his racing feet.

He hit the steel supports and hunkered down.

A container was swung from thick chains. One side was open. Against the other side the form of Brownie showed, clearly in the pearly light. Brownie was spreadeagled against the wall of the container, tied tightly, spreadeagled blasphemously like a living sacrifice.

'Brownie!'

As Doyle watched the red dot appeared on the wall over Brownie's head. It travelled down the man's face, over his shirt, centred on his heart.

'For Crissake, Ray! He'll kill me!'

Preston's voice hammered the still air.

'Not him, Doyle. I want you. Now!'

The red dot jumped sharply to the ground before the open side of the container. The unmistakable rattle of a 180 cracked out and bullets raked the ground, driving dust up in evil little spurts. Brownie quivered to the gunfire and the strikes.

'Do something, Ray!'

Doyle looked around. The yards, the cranes, the lines of containers, the smell of oil and metal, everything seemed to whirl about him. He swallowed down and took a fresh grip on his pistol. 'Let him go, Preston.'

Preston's voice gloated with triumph. For this he had planned and waited. 'Your choice, Doyle. You can cut him down – or I will . . .'

Desperately, Doyle cast about for that tell-tale glint of red light. In the angle of an engine shed, high, a glint appeared. He focused up; but nothing moved there. The sun shafted a streamer of gold through the greyness and obscured Doyle's vision. He looked away, blinking. Where in hell was the bastard?

That dominating, hectoring, demanding voice hammered out again. 'I want you, Doyle. Not him!'

The hateful red dot sprang into being above Brownie's head. A burst of gunfire raked across the container. Splinters of wood showered away, raw and yellow. Brownie choked and slobbered. He gargled and groaned and managed to croak out: 'Ray!'

The way Doyle saw it, he had no option, professional or no damned professional.

Keeping as low as he could he raced across the intervening ground, ducked under the metal supports, clawed his way up to the container. The ropes holding Brownie had been tied hard and then yanked cruelly tighter still. The man's wrists were bloodless. He stared at Doyle as though seeing a ghost.

A rattle began. The container swayed. Doyle shot a look up. The chain was hauling up, trundling through the pulley. They were being hoisted up into the air.

A line of fire raked the ground before the container and Doyle hunkered back. The dust puffed, acrid in the flat air.

'He's up there,' Brownie said, half-choked.

Doyle looked up to the engine shed.

The figure of Preston appeared on the roof, standing up. He looked like a vulture perched on a cactus waiting for the dead to yield up their eyeballs.

'Enjoying yourself, Doyle?' he shouted across the intervening distance. 'I am.'

With a deliberateness that chilled, Preston lifted the 180 and took aim.

With a final desperate wrench Doyle got the ropes undone and the imprisoned wrists slipped through. Brownie yelped as the circulation started to strike daggers into him. Doyle shoved him hard towards the end of the container.

He showed what he wanted done and the two men began heaving their weight about, managing to start the container swinging on its chains.

The slab-sided container swung around ponderously.

Brownie gasped: 'Why don't you shoot the bastard?'

Doyle lifted his gun in disgust. 'Sure, if he'd come a little closer. Otherwise might as well spit in the wind.'

They went on heaving at the container, making it spin.

'Don't you ever,' Brownie told Doyle, 'ever ask me to work for you again, will you?'

Preston vanished from view. But the container reached the maximum twist on the chains. It hovered. Then, inexorably, it began to twist back as the chains unwound.

In moments the gaping open side of the coffin-like box would swing around, revealing them to Preston and the deadly red dot.

The ex-Detective Superintendent relished his work. He loved it. This was what he hungered for, the destruction of the last man who had ruined his life. He smiled. He lifted the 180 as the container swung, and swung, the chains slowly unwinding. In a couple of moments he would align that red dot over Doyle's forehead and blow the top of his head off as he had blown Maurice Richards's head off . . .

A voice, a loud voice, a very loud voice through a loud-hailer battered across the scene. George Cowley's voice.

'Look down, Preston. *Look down!*'

Preston blinked irritatedly as a light shone in his eyes. Then he went rigid as the voice boomed at him. He looked down.

Red spot hovered over his heart.

He couldn't believe . . .

He looked up, swiftly, raging. A police launch wallowed in the river. Cowley stood braced, the loud hailer lifted. At his side Bodie crouched, and in his capable fists a 180 smg, twin to the one held by Preston, pointed up unerringly.

'Gently, now, Preston. Put the gun down. Slowly.'

Preston began to put the gun down as though hypnotised.

The chains untwisted. The container spun around

presenting the open side to his vicious gaze. Doyle and Brownie crouched in the container, staring up at him. Preston stopped putting the gun down. For a moment he stood, quivering with the trapped feelings of a wild beast in a snare, then he started to lift the gun.

'Don't be a fool, Preston. Drop it!'

The gun dropped from Preston's nerveless fingers. He was horribly conscious of the red spot over his heart. The 180 clattered over the roof and fell with a thud and a spurt of dust between the tracks.

Doyle and Brownie stood up.

Doyle was smiling and stowing his gun away.

Brownie expelled a deep and long-held breath.

'You fellahs cut it a bit fine.'

'Yeah,' said Doyle, slapping the gun safely away. 'Beats sailing . . .'

The Gothic architecture of the old swimming baths that served as the CI5 action-course HQ still lifted awkwardly from the derelict area. The crumbling houses continued to crumble. Bangs and flashes and spurts of smoke erupted from the ruins and rubble as toughly professional instructors chased green trainees around the course.

The place looked the same. But events had taken place that would make the place never seem the same again to Bodie – and, especially – to Doyle.

Against a rubbled wall a spindly metal table stood with a covering of green baize. On the table the two 180s lay, side by side.

Cowley spoke briskly to Bodie and Doyle.

'It's certainly an impressive weapon.'

Bodie nodded: 'You can say that again, sir. Half the time you don't even need to fire it. As soon as your criminal or your terrorist sees the red dot on him, he knows he's got no chance, and gives in.'

'As long,' Doyle pointed out, 'as he knows what it is, of course.'

'Well,' said Bodie, only a little huffed, 'your mate Preston did, didn't he?'

'I still want a full written evaluation from you.' Cowley insisted on routine when it was routine like this. 'Including its efficiency.'

'Well, sir,' said Bodie, 'I think Preston proved that for us. He shot Richards – inside his pub – while he was half a mile away on the other side of the river.'

'No wonder he stopped when you lined the other one up on him.' Doyle could still feel the unwinding swing of that blasted container, and the way the landscape revolved around him, bringing that maniac Preston and his lethal 180 nearer and nearer for the final shot. The shot that would not miss because the red dot would stand out vividly on Doyle's forehead.

Cowley turned to Bodie. 'Your arms dealer friend may have some explaining to do. I want to know how he got hold of a 180 for you.'

'Oh, didn't I tell you, sir?' Bodie was all eager innocence. 'That's not a real gun. It's only a dummy, to demonstrate the sight. Good, isn't it?'

He picked up one of the guns. They were alike as two tins of baked beans on a shelf. He aimed it casually at the row of targets nearby and idly clicked the trigger off.

The targets burst into a myriad shards of flying wood splinters and shreds of canvas under the storm of lead.

Bodie froze . . . shaken rigid.

Doyle almost collapsed . . .. holding down his mirth.

Cowley almost exploded . . . blasted pair of clowns!

He turned on one of his two ace agents, frigid with outraged authority.

'Bodie!'

Chapter Nine

The railways run a comfortable and fast service – well, most of the time – and that means maintenance. The yards up past York Road through Camden Town might not be the jungles they were once said to be; but at night with the big arcs cutting wedges of brilliance against the black and the ghostly echoing noises of men at work, the smell of diesel and grease and the choky metallic stinks all about, they were what a city could offer in the jungle stakes.

Bodie and Doyle walked softly along the tracks Bodie said were the ones the arrangement called for, as usual.

They passed the blue and grey coaches, lean efficient transport animals. Doyle stuck a thumb at the nearest.

'This one?'

'Yes,' said Bodie. Then, as Doyle started to reach out for the door, Bodie cut in swiftly: 'No. First Class! Parker's got delusions of grandeur.'

Further along the First Class showed the long, low windows of the Mark III Inter-City. Bodie opened the end door and swung up from the ballast, and Doyle silently followed.

Parker had set the meet up in the usual way, ringing the phone three times, then once, then twice more, so that Bodie, amusedly checking Doyle's instinctive move to lift the receiver, knew who, when and where.

Now Parker sat hunched in the corner of the First Class, wary, his coat pulled up, his long sideburns giving his narrow face the look of a borzoi. His lips were somewhat thick for so lugubrious a face, and they shone with spittle.

His shoes were black and highly polished, with a rime of the railyard's grime.

'You weren't followed?'

'Am I ever?' Bodie made it light. You had to handle Parker with kid gloves. Now Parker stared suspiciously at Doyle.

'Who's he?'

Bodie told him. 'What have you got for me?'

'The goods, I hope. Heard it in the club tonight. I'm well liked there, you know. It's the real McCoy. The Coogans. Big John – and young Paul . . . If you want him.'

'I,' said Bodie, echoing the words of the chief of C15, George Cowley, 'want 'em both.'

'Then you've got 'em.'

'When?'

'Tonight!'

Arrangements for the raid were put in hand the moment the agents contacted Cowley. The cars rolled through the night, destination, the luxurious and secluded house of ex-boxer John Coogan. Bodie drove the eleven-year-old Jaguar which he continued to operate out of the C15 motor pool. Cowley sat alongside and Doyle hunched forward in the rear seats.

'It's a big drop. Maybe ten pounds of uncut heroin.'

'Coogan's chancing that – under his own roof?' Cowley did not disbelieve Bodie; but it was an incredible event.

Doyle smiled. 'That's the nice part. The offer came suddenly. Original buyer got busted, leaving ten pounds of uncut floating. And the Coogans moved in.'

Bodie amplified the deal. 'It has to be their house – wasn't time to arrange anything else.'

Very softly and with great meaning, Cowley said: 'I've wanted the Coogan Brothers for a long time.'

Bodie swung the wheel to bring the car off the road.

With great satisfaction, he said: 'And now you've got 'em.'

A few stars pricked out; but massy clouds drove across

and shadowed the high wall and the ornate wrought-iron gates. Coogan's town house was a veritable mansion, secluded, standing in its own extensive grounds, with distant traffic muted by trees and hedges. Only a very wealthy man could afford to run a place like this in this day and age. And the Coogans, the two brothers, John and Paul, were wealthy. Cowley knew how they acquired their money, and he didn't like it. He had seen too many ruined kids, hollow-cheeked, red-eyed, whimpering for a shot, destroyed.

The agents from CI5 moved carefully up the curving drive. The house lifted four-square, with a turret, very Italianate. The front door of solid oak, studded with bronze bolt-heads, could prove an obstacle. Cowley nodded.

Doyle and two of the broadest-shouldered and huskiest of the CI5 men rushed. They hit the door. They did not bounce. The door burst inwards. It had not been bolted, merely on the latch. Cowley took that as an omen of good fortune for the night. Doyle and the others rushed headlong inside. Bodie stood a little off, away from the main action . . .

Frank Williams – he had been conditioned out of being called Arthur a long time ago – rounded the far corner of the house. He heard the smash as the front door broke in. Williams was a burly, tough, physical man, devoted to the Coogans. He stood night watch with a shotgun.

Frank saw the dark mass of men rushing through the door – he saw that beautiful door all smashed and askew from the hinges – and he let out a yell and jumped forward. He jerked the shotgun to his shoulder. He would shoot these bastards breaking in – by God! they weren't the first in gang wars Frank had seen off, not by a long chalk. His finger tightened on the triggers.

A long and lean arm shot from the shadows. The hand clamped into a fist around the barrels and as the shotgun boom-boomed the charges went skittering up into the trees.

Bodie brought his other fist around in a haymaker that sledged alongside Frank's jaw. Frank went over. He hit the ground like a sack of best nuts. He did not get up.

Still gripping the shotgun, Bodie swung back to the house.

A considerable hullaballoo was going on inside, and lights were springing into life, shining through window after window as the CI5 made their way through the house. Looking up, Bodie saw a first floor window open, glinting oddly from reflected light. The mis-shapen shadow of a man appeared, galvanised, jerking. With a yell the man leaped, hit the flowerbeds, staggered, ran crazily for the parked Triumph TR7, trailing a fine standard rose caught around his shoulders.

Bodie started running to cut the man off. As the fugitive sprinted across the lights spilling from the shattered front door he was revealed as Paul Coogan. Paul was much nearer the TR7 and he leaped in and the motor burst into life. Paul gunned the car away, spurting gravel, speeded down the drive.

Bodie hauled up, fuming. A dark car accelerated out of the shadows and hurtled forward. Doug Waters was driving. He hit the TR7 beam on, rammed the sports car, sent it skidding sideways. Paul was flung about like a rag doll.

Doug leaped out and ran to the stopped car. Then, easily, he reached in and switched off the motor. Then he put his capable hand on Paul Coogan's shoulder.

Turning away, satisfied, Bodie saw the CI5 men appearing from the house, bringing John Coogan. A big man, about 45, he wore a floral silk dressing gown that must have cut swathes through the ranks of the local ladies. His hair was still immaculate. The agents led him across and picked up his brother on the way. Paul was around 30, lighter in build than the block-busting physique of John. He wore a sweater and slacks, and his fair hair was ruffled and fell forward in a yellow curve over his forehead. He looked apprehensive, not scared.

Bodie moved on and joined Cowley and Doyle and the others as they emerged from the front door.

'We haven't found anything yet,' said Cowley in his

tombstone-grinding voice. 'But we will. *You* will.'

Cowley, grim-faced, moved away to his car. Bodie and Doyle exchanged the old 'heyho, here we go again' look, and went back into the house. The smashed front door looked pathetic, but the bronze bolt-heads glittered splendidly.

CI5 were using a temporary headquarters, part of a derelict warehouse complex with rooms and stairways that afforded them all the spartan accommodation they needed. They had done good work from here, and the atmosphere was brisk and no-nonsense, get-on-with-the-job. The Coogan brothers were taken through and up the stairs, being pushed on every now and then by the agents in an almost resigned way, little 'get-moving shoves. John entered his room, which was hardly dignified by the term cell, with a swagger. Paul went into the large bleak interrogation room in a more docile frame of mind. He stood looking about, and he shivered. His eyes widened as he saw the graffiti on the wall. Among the obscene words one particular graffito caught his attention – his somewhat alarmed attention. THEY'RE ALL MURDERING BASTARDS. Paul Coogan read that with a touch of trepidation.

As the doors shut, John bellowed out, his voice ringing and hollow in the bleak corridor: 'You hear me, Pauly? Not one word!' Paul heard, and shivered. 'Not one word! Whatever they do.'

Early the following morning – very early – with the freshness of dawn still perfuming the garden of Coogan's opulent house, David Merlin brought his Daimler in through the wrought iron gates and halted by the shattered front door. He saw the rammed TR7, and his keen dark eyes took in the evidence of the struggle of the previous night. A slight man, impeccably dressed, expertly-groomed, around 45, his features held an almost saturnine cast. His thin lips could cut into the most devastating sneer of contempt – a most powerful weapon in his armoury – and among the criminal fraternity he was known as a man who knew which side his bread was buttered. Among his clients he had often felt he numbered the Coogans as his most valuable. He'd kept them out of trouble in the past – but this latest bust looked more ominous than he cared for.

'You should see the *inside* of the house – ' came Frank Williams's voice, and Merlin turned to see the interestingly coloured bruise, yellow and green and purple, along Frank's face where Bodie had hit him. 'A typhoon would've been kinder. I sent for you, Mr Merlin, because Big John said always to send for you if there was trouble.'

'You did the right thing. They didn't find anything?'

Frank Williams just smiled. That hurt him, and he winced.

Cowley wasn't smiling as he browbeat Doyle and Bodie, and it still hurt him.

'Nothing!'

'Not a damned thing.' The warehouse HQ around them seemed to hold its bricks and mortar breath, waiting for Cowley's explosion. Bodie hurriedly added: 'We went over the place with a fine toothcomb.'

'Twice.' Doyle did not look happy. 'With *two* toothcombs. Infrared and sniffer dogs – '

With that crinkle thinning his lips dangerously, Bodie said: 'Parker gave us a bum steer.'

'He's been reliable before,' Cowley said.

Doyle pushed a hand through his curly hair. 'I reckon someone outbid the Coogans.' Well, that made sense. 'Someone got in first. We didn't find it because it was never there to find.'

'Right.' Cowley gestured. 'We've still got the Coogans. Let's have a quiet chat with them, shall we?'

The three went along to the room in which John Coogan had spent a truculent night. Big, contemptuous of them, he glowered as they came in. The table was clean and bare, the chair half-pushed back. John sneered. 'Which one's going to do the hitting?' He looked at Doyle. 'Not you, not enough weight.' He brooded on Bodie for a moment. 'And you – you'd break your hand on me.' He stuck his jaw out, blue with bristle. 'No glass *there*.' He pulled aside the silk robe to expose his abdomen, a ridged and hard expanse of muscle. He banged his own guts. 'And this. Like a rock. My kid brother works out on it some mornings. Fifty-three bouts when I was in the ring, and nobody ever put me down. If you're the best you can do – you're not good enough.'

Very gently, in his plummy voice, Cowley told him: 'You shouldn't believe every rumour you hear, Coogan. There's going to be no hitting.'

John drew his lips back. 'No?' Abruptly he whirled, snatched up the wooden chair and smashed it shatteringly against the wall. 'Somebody might have heard that. Then it's your word against mine, isn't it?'

Cowley said: 'Sit down, Coogan.'

John stared challengingly back at the chief of CI5.

'Sit down.'

The stare John bent on Cowley was returned with a calm steadfastness that made John consider. He turned and sat down.

A banging began, faint but solid, thumping through the wall. Paul Coogan's voice sounded muffled. 'Hey, hey, hey!'

Cowley jerked his head. 'See to him.'

Bodie and Doyle – aware that Cowley could look after himself – nodded and went out of the room smartly.

They bashed into the large and somehow hostile area of the interrogation room to find Paul Coogan banging his shoe on the table and banging it against the wall, in a one-two that carried menacing overtones of the rataplan of war drums. They stopped stock still and looked at him.

Paul stopped his banging and glared up, his yellow forelock falling over his eyes. 'I heard. You've been working him over – and now it's my turn?' The partners said nothing. 'Well, you won't find me any easier than him. John can take it and so can I.'

This amused Bodie. 'Oh – I don't think you're ready to play in the big league yet.'

'So,' added Doyle. 'Just be a good boy, eh? And when we're ready for you – '

Breathlessly, the colour flooding his face, Paul burst out: 'I'm ready now.' He sounded like a lad facing the dentist's drill.

'Yeah, yeah,' said Doyle. He turned away, anxious to get back to Cowley now that nothing serious was going on in here.

'Just try me,' shouted Paul, incensed by their attitude of nonchalance, the way they were ignoring his bravado.

The feeling of denigration, of being a nothing, overwhelmed Paul Coogan. He jumped for Doyle and lashed out, a wild punch that caught Doyle behind the ear, stingingly. Doyle swung about. He felt his own rage mounting; but he controlled it, shoved it back down where it belonged. His face set and his voice was like ice. 'Don't push your luck.'

He turned away at once, not wishing to get into a slanging match. Paul Coogan couldn't leave well alone. A man who had grown up and lived in the shadow of his brother, he desperately wanted to exert himself for himself, to show these supercilious bastards that he was just as tough as Big John. He leaped for Doyle and started in swinging savage punches. His blows hurt.

The ex-policeman lurched away and, as Paul followed, still swinging wildly, viciously, Doyle turned and leaned in. Doyle threw one punch. Just the one. A short jab to the body. A single short controlled punch. He made it quick and clean.

Paul staggered back. His hands spread and then gripped in over his stomach. His face slackened, and then tautened, and then slackened again. Bodie and Doyle, after one look, went out. Paul remained clutching his abdomen, curiously still.

The Minister did not like being up this early; but he had called in the chief of CI5 and Cowley was here, in the office among the big ornate desk and the functional filing cabinets and the humidor and the telephones – the red one a little to one side. Now the Minister leaned forward and regarded George Cowley with the speculative eye that took in all the signs he did not wish to see. 'David Merlin.'

Cowley reacted. 'Merlin! That shyster –'

'He lives up to his namesake. He's a legal wizard, has friends at court – and represents the Coogan brothers.'

'Represents!' snorted Cowley. 'Does their dirty business you mean.'

'David Merlin is a highly respected lawyer –'

'Not by me!'

The Minister waved an elegantly-suited arm. 'Nor me, George. But he's raising an awful stink. He's alleging damage to private property – search without warrant –'

'Without warrant? You know the terms of my brief.'

'Yes, George.' The Minister's voice was quiet, soft, and carried a tone that brought Cowley's antennae up, quivering. 'And it is that brief that is endangered at this moment. I know what you do – and why. But ultimately we must answer to the Government of this country, and they in turn to the voters.' He put it, harshly, now. 'Can you hold the Coogans? Do you have a case?'

'Not at the moment, no. John Coogan is a thug. Drugs, extortion, prostitution – given a few hours' interrogation, and –'

'Then you must release them immediately. In the eyes of the great British public, John Coogan is a revered athlete, and he's up for an OBE. Until you can prove otherwise . . . ? No. George, I'm not asking you. I'm telling you. Get them away and perhaps I can hold the cork on a fizz bottle very close to bursting.'

Orders were orders. Cowley knew it was no use fuming; but he fumed, anyway. John Coogan let them all know the contempt in which he held them, and took delight in telling them he'd known they couldn't hold him. Bodie and Doyle went along to the interrogation room to fetch his brother Paul.

Paul sat at the table, slumped over. Bodie said: 'All right. The cage is open. You can fly away now.'

Paul did not move. Bodie gripped his shoulder.

'Come on, sonny . . .'

Shaking the still figure, Bodie saw Paul's arm slide off the table and dangle like a piece of chewed string. He bent quickly. 'Coogan . . . ?' Bodie felt the pulse, and, after a long-enough moment, straightened and looked at his partner. His face was unreadable.

'Doyle – he's dead!'

Up on the wall the graffito read THEY'RE ALL MURDERING BASTARDS.

Wheels were set in motion. At his house with all its luxury mocking him with his loss, John Coogan told David Merlin exactly what he wanted done. As Jill – the latest in a long line of young and attractive girls – nubile, as John liked to say – played tennis against herself with a tethered ball, John spoke in a harsh and vicious tone.

'I want them, Merlin. I want them all. Cowley – his organisation. Whoever killed Pauly.'

'It's going to be very expensive, John.'

'Just get them out from behind their badge, break 'em, make 'em ordinary people again. You take care of *that* – and then one night, down some dark street, *I'll* take care of *them* my way.'

Merlin nodded and set more wheels in motion. Once more the Minister called George Cowley in. This time the explosion was nearer the surface; but bottled up, kept in, contained.

'A court of inquiry?' said Cowley, sitting down, holding to the edge of the chair. 'With questions and answers in the open? The strength of this organisation is its anonymity –'

'And people are saying it has *too much* strength.' He showed Cowley a morning paper of impeccable quality. 'Look, George. "CI5. Brutality? A Big Brother State?" It's been agreed. The court of inquiry will convene on Thursday.'

Cowley sat, stunned. He heard the Minister saying: 'Who will you want as counsel? To present your side of the affair?'

That roused George Cowley. 'Counsel?' he said, lifting his head, his face harsh in the desk light. 'My God. I formed this organisation and I'll answer for it!'

'I thought you'd say that. And I agree. No one is better equipped to defend CI5 than yourself. But, George, you understand you won't just be defending the rights and wrongs of the Coogan issue.' The Minister's voice betrayed the depth of his concern. 'But the continued existence of the whole department?'

'I understand.'

'And you'll be up against very tough opposition.'

'David Merlin.'

'He'll mastermind it, I'm sure.' The Minister's face showed what he thought of Merlin, and could not admit to. 'But at the actual inquiry . . . ? He'll need someone beyond reproach, someone utterly sincere, utterly committed. I think,' the Minister finished as though pronouncing a death sentence. 'I think you'll be up against Geraldine Mather.'

Cowley's chin went up. He'd formed CI5 and he could point to exemplary work the department had successfully done; he was not prepared to sit idly by and watch his work, work for the good of the nation, destroyed.

The wheels continued to revolve as David Merlin acted as the Minister so shrewdly suspected. After all, Geraldine Mather was the currently fashionable barrister, intense, dedicated and highly successful. About 30, she was strikingly attractive with her slender yet full figure, her sleek dark hair and her mobile mouth, and she was well aware of her own beauty and traded on it unashamedly. Her eyes held the bright intensity causes are made of. She would have been one of the first to smash a window or chain herself to the railings outside the Houses of Parliament seventy years ago. Now she studied the brief assiduously.

Her office was spare and businesslike, and Merlin, sitting across the desk from her, watching her as she read, steepled his fingertips, content to let her go her own successful way.

Geraldine Mather looked up. Her face frowned and those brilliant eyes still held the impressions of the depositions.

'It's hideous – unthinkable. It has to be exposed, and stopped. Yes, Mr Merlin, I'd be pleased to prosecute this case.'

Merlin said, swiftly: *'A court of inquiry,* Miss Mather. There will be no actual *prosecution.'*

Miss Mather's smile twisted those mobile lips and did unflattering things to her face. 'There will be – the way I intend to present it.' Merlin felt the pleasure at her tone. 'Are there any legal ground rules as to *where* the inquiry will be held?'

Merlin felt surprised. 'A room in some convenient location, I suppose . . . '

'That's what I thought.' The lop-sided and bitter smile remained and the eyes brightened as Miss Mather stood up. 'So let's play our first ace.'

The wheels revolved again and this time they brought the Minister in person in his car to the warehouse complex currently being used as a temporary CI5 HQ. He walked with Cowley towards the battered old warehouse block.

'Here!' said Cowley. 'She wants to hold the inquiry here?'

'In the room in which Paul Coogan died.'

'For pity's sake . . . '

'Her argument,' the Minister said, feeling for Cowley, 'is that it will save time should the court wish to view the – er – scene of the crime. If we don't agree she'll only make further capital out of it.'

'And if we do, she's already ten points ahead on sheer emotional appeal.' They walked on for a few paces. Cowley persisted in his stubborn belief in himself, his men and his organisation. 'Let her have the room – she doesn't frighten me.'

'She should.' At the Minister's tone Cowley looked very sharply at him, very sharply indeed. The Minister was no chicken. 'A good healthy respect, at least. She's out to break CI5, George. And you with it.'

Wheels carrying a more sombre burden brought Paul Coogan's coffin to the graveyard. As usual this wet summer the weather rained dismally down, glistening on marble statuary and headstones, setting puddles in the gravel walks, soaking the trees and grass and pathetic flowers, making the freshly-turned mud shine and smell with that special smell of mud in rain.

John Coogan's face froze grimly with grief as the ceremony went through. Frank Williams was there, looking uncomfortable. The vicar droned on through the words, trying to shield the Book from the rain. The shining mud glistened and the wet raw smell of the earth caught in Frank's throat.

'It doesn't seem right,' Frank whispered, half to himself. 'Keeping all Pauly's friends away. It doesn't seem right.'

Softly as he spoke, John heard. His own voice just reached Frank as the rain pattered softly down.

'His friends? French Charley and Nosher and Mad Harry? All those ugly mugs staring out of the newspapers? We've got to do like Merlin said. We've got to be respectable.' John looked at the mound of wreaths with their sodden ribbons and labels. 'Anyway, they didn't forget him.' He hunched up the shoulders of his expensive black coat against the rain. 'Check the labels later, and if anyone did forget him they'll hear from me.'

When the inevitable reporters crowded in John was all ready for them. 'I'm not going to let them cover it up. They're covering my brother with dirt – he was just twenty-nine years old, cut down.'

One reporter blurted out: 'Are you suggesting it was deliberately done?'

'I know it was.' Again John hunched his black shoulders where each rain drop clung to a fibre, glinting. 'And I mean to prove it. No, no, they're not going to cover this one up!'

He shouldered his way off to the waiting car, long and black and shining, and climbed in. Frank came to sit at his side.

'Didn't overdo it, did I?' demanded John, not looking at Frank, gazing at the drifting lines of rain.

'Just right.'

'I'm bothered, Franky.' John Coogan's gloved hands

began to twist together, ruthlessly, as though grinding a hated enemy's neck. 'When they bust in? Right time, right place, everything . . .'

'If that stuff hadn't gone to a higher bidder,' said Frank and his relief was obvious. 'We'd have been done.'

'Yeah.' The hands twisted and gripped and the brooding eyes looked out into the rain. 'So who tipped them off? I'd like to know, Franky.'

Doyle's flat looked different from its usual cheerful cleanliness and neatness, for all the piled lumber of living usually scattered about. An air of despondency cloaked the pad, and the author of that despondency lay on the settee, face up, moodily surveying the miniscule cracks of the ceiling. Doyle just lay there, hardly moving, breathing lightly, sunk in apathy. Bodie called him, standing by the punchball on its heavy stand.

'Doyle?'

No answer.

'Doyle!'

Ray Doyle just lay there.

Bodie walked across and, concerned, looked down on his recumbent partner. 'Doyle – you all right?' He didn't like that glazed look in the eyes . . . 'Thought you'd be shaved and showered by now, belly full of organic foods – and working out.' Here Bodie gave the punch ball a playful whack.

'What for?' As Bodie gaped at him, he went on: 'What for, I said. "Working out" – what for? So I can rupture someone else's spleen?'

Doyle rolled off the settee, turned his back, and walked away. Bodie regarded him with those eyebrows of his drawn down. He'd have to tread verree verree carefully with Doyle hereabouts . . .

'It was an accident.'

'Yeah,' said Doyle, not turning. 'He ran right on to my fist.'

Very patiently Bodie went over it again. 'Look, I was there. He came at you. You turned, and . . . It could have happened anywhere. Pub brawl, anywhere. It could have happened to anyone.'

'But it didn't happen to anyone.' The ugly note in Doyle's voice shook Bodie. 'It happened to me.'

'You only hit him once.'

Doyle swung about, his face taut and somehow tightly knit and yet long, so unlike his usual cheerful roundness. 'You mean, if I'd hit him twice, I could have killed him twice, is that what you mean?'

As he spoke he vented his anger with a tremendous punch and the punchball whanged back and forwards, vibrating.

Doyle stared. 'D'you see what they've made of me? Do you see what they're making of us? I'm angry – so what do I do? I hit out. Without thinking – without thinking, Bodie!' He took a breath, shaking. 'It scares the Hell out of me.'

Bodie regarded his partner with feelings he admitted were those of deep concern, of exasperation, and of loyalty. At last, speaking in a clipped way he hoped would get through, he said: 'I came here because the old man's got a job for us.'

'Not me.' Doyle's bitterness made Bodie wince. 'I'm suspended – remember?'

'Me too.' Doyle swung about, through all the pain in him intrigued by the meaning of the remark. Bodie went on: 'Material witness. I saw you beat that innocent young man to death.'

The moment he spoke, the moment he saw the way Doyle's face twitched, the way his head went down, Bodie knew he had made a bad mistake. Doyle's terrible inner anger spilled out.

'Bodie, don't make jokes. I'm telling you, don't make jokes, or so help me . . .'

He bought his clenched fist up before him, shaking, glaring at his partner, his face a twin to the fist that shook under Bodie's nose. Then, suddenly, he realised what he was doing, just what his reflexes had betrayed his body into doing.

Bodie saw that. He saw the quivering fist, he saw the sheer wash of tired anger draw the life from Doyle. His own anger flared.

'How else do I get through to you? The old man needs us. I've never seen him like this before. He's fighting for his life – and he needs us. We owe him something – don't we?'

'We?' Doyle half-turned away and dragged his fist down, shoving his unclenched hand behind his back, as though shoving it out of existence. 'What happened to your "always look after number one" credo?'

Speaking evenly, Bodie said: 'Don't do as I say – do as I do.' Bodie stared back as Doyle looked at him. For a moment they glared at each other, the emotions twining and clogging between them. Then, finally, Bodie who operated on a hair-trigger most of the time, a hair-trigger he could almost always keep perfectly under control, began to lose patience. 'Okay. Okay, I'll handle it alone. And leave you to wallow in your own self pity.'

Doyle broke in sharply: 'Since when did you ever handle anything alone?'

Bodie saw a sign, a welcome sign, and he let Doyle ponder for just a moment, before he cracked back. 'Since when did you?'

Now, as they looked at each other, the old camaraderie returned. They'd always emotionally slug it out, one with the other; but when, as the croupiers said, the chips were down, they were a pair.

'Why us?' demanded Doyle. 'If we're both suspended?'

'Because Parker is my pigeon. Our pigeon.' Bodie's face indicated his feelings of impending action. 'Henry Parker, informer. He's dropped out of sight.'

'I don't blame him, with Coogan still running loose.'

'Just the same, he set this ball rolling. Cowley needs to talk to him.' Bodie turned away, clearly heading for the door.

For a moment Doyle stared after him. Then he reached for his jacket. 'Okay,' he said. 'Okay.'

Chapter Ten

Geraldine Mather had the advantage of possessing a brilliant mind as well as a luscious body and a beautiful face. Her attractiveness by its very openness might have repelled men concerned over the razor-edged sharpness of her brain. But she had worked hard and done all the right things and was a popular diner at the regular dinners in. There were those who said she was too sharp by half; but usually they were those who had attempted her and failed.

Now she went with David Merlin to view the scene of the coming court of inquiry. Miss Mather had had to fight her way through to become a successful barrister, and her family had loyally supported her all the way. Injustice inflamed her. As they came in she saw workmen in white coveralls busy about the room. The size of the room, its bleakness, the atmosphere of corruption and violence that seemed to hang in the trapped air caught at her throat.

One of the workmen lifted an aerosol and began to spray white paint over the wall. The jet of whiteness sliced long sweeping curves of fresh cleanliness over the walls and the graffiti. The paint reached out to obliterate THEY'RE ALL MURDERING BASTARDS and Miss Geraldine Mather, in a firm, hard voice, called : 'NO.'

She walked up to the compact, sandy-haired man whose lined, square face indicated a lot of living. She noticed the intelligence of his eyes, and filed that away, along with the firmness and yet sensibility of his mouth. He walked, she noticed, with a slight limp.

'You are Cowley?' She turned her smooth dark head to

look meaningfully at Merlin. 'I'm glad we came by. I thought you might try to do this.'

Cowley said: 'Do what?'

'Remove or destroy evidence.'

She might have accused Cowley of trying to nobble the Queen's favourite for the Derby, or for drowning new-born babies. 'What!'

'I must insist that this room remains exactly as it is.'

Miss Mather was perfectly cool. It was clear she knew exactly what she was doing.

'I was just trying,' Cowley explained, 'to make it more habitable –'

'You do not regard it as habitable at this moment?' Miss Mather interrupted ruthlessly. 'Yet it is quite habitable enough for conducting your interrogations in?'

For a moment Cowley regarded this formidable woman. Then, in his smooth plummy voice, he told her: 'Very well – but you won't mind standing for a whole day then?'

'Oh, I anticipated the inquiry lasting several days. And of course, chairs must be provided.' She indicated the cheap wooden chairs the workmen had been taking out and replacing with upholstered office chairs. '*This* kind of chair. I want the inquiry board to know the kind of comfort you offer your unfortunate prisoners. I want them to feel it in their backsides.'

Cowley's sharp lunge had been met with an even sharper riposte. Merlin followed Mather out, and he felt very pleased with this female legal eagle. Coogan ought to be pleased, too. As for George Cowley –

'Old fool,' said Merlin as they went along the corridor.

Miss Mather favoured him with a cutting look. 'If you think that – then you are the fool. No, Cowley is many things . . . But a fool he is not.'

The day of the court of inquiry opened with a sharp shower of rain that slicked up pavements and drove people hurrying along from doorway to doorway. Well, there was nothing unusual in that, this year; but Bodie, for one, could have done with a nice drop of sunshine to cheer things up. They sat on a couple of the chairs lined up in the corridor for witnesses. There was a deal of activity. Clothes held that musky rain-sodden smell, and there was a lot of umbrella shaking. Reporters were allowed in and they shouldered through in their rough and ready way, agog to witness the redoubtable Geraldine Mather in action again, and, each according to his own beliefs, wanting CI5 to be crucified or left to get on with the job of hunting criminals.

All the reporters were checked by Carter, a CI5 agent, on the door of the interrogation room. John Coogan and Frank Williams walked in. John looked in an expansive mood, his dark desires for revenge overcoming the last vestiges of grief. David Merlin and Mather walked together, the legal brains, and as Bodie clocked Geraldine Mather his eyebrows rose. She looked cool and beautiful and could have passed for any one of the many voluptuous models Bodie was wont to pass his time with.

Eyeing her and speaking softly to his partner, Bodie said: 'She can prosecute me any time.'

The group broke up as John and Frank crossed to take seats in the corridor, whilst Merlin and Mather passed Carter at the door and entered the interrogation room.

The tables and chairs had been ranged around in a fair simulacrum of a court. Merlin and Mather made their way to the table indicated, sat down and began producing papers from their briefcases. At another small table sat Cowley and the Minister. A chair sat front and centre, empty, awaiting its transient freight of witnesses. The reporters clustered at the far end, attempting to keep quiet. A somewhat longer table faced the others, and here sat the presiding judge, Judge Smith, and the other two members of the board. Cowley had been warned about them by the Minister, very concerned, the night before.

'Judge Smith,' the Minister had said. 'No problem there. He's only interested in the pure facts of the matter. There's Anthony Stennard – '

'He's a fair man. Got a good mind, too. He won't be swayed by pure emotion.'

'And there is McKay – Harold McKay, the man who

has opposed CI5 since its inception. He'll be seeking to make political capital out of this. He'll try to get it over your broken back.'

The court settled, and Cowley regarded the three men of the board levelly, seeking to read some emotion in their faces. Judge Smith banged his gavel as the court settled. Silence.

Judge Smith introduced the board and then explained the facts of his warrant. 'I would like to point out to the members of the press that they are here as a matter of courtesy rather than a matter of right. It may well be that certain testimony will be subject to the Official Secrets Act, and that this court will instruct that such testimony must not be published –'

Geraldine Mather rose to her feet. The silence as the Judge waited for her words was a clear and chilling indication of the respect this woman evoked. 'I reserve the right,' said Miss Mather in her most formidable tones, 'to question or protest any such instruction, Mr President.'

'Miss Mather.' Judge Smith regarded her with his usual deep courtesy. 'May I remind you that this is not a court such as you are accustomed to. Ultimately, we have no judicial powers. We can only make findings and recommendations –'

'I am aware, Mr President, that this is not a court of law.' She looked quite deliberately at the expectant reporters. 'But I hope we shall find it is a court of justice.'

That got to them. The reports of the proceedings would not fail to record this telling opening statement, even if the pretty girl who was the court stenographer, sitting at the table by the clerk of the court, did not react as the others did.

Judge Smith cleared his throat. 'I shall now read the charge.'

With the preliminaries out of the way Geraldine Mather rose. There were no doubts in her mind. She was dedicated to justice and to liberty, and she was completely and passionately sincere in her beliefs. She eyed the court for a moment, and then began speaking in an easy tone, warming up gently, well knowing the devastating armoury she could bring to bear.

'I would like to begin my address with an apology. These surroundings are far from comfortable but it was *my* suggestion the inquiry be held here. I wanted you all to sample the hospitality offered by CI5 to their unfortunate suspects, to try and imagine what it must be like to be held *incommunicado* in a place like this. What would run through your mind . . . ?'

Accidentally-on-purpose Miss Mather had paced to the wall bearing the particular graffito she had selected as epitomising what went on here. She rested her hand on the wall, below the sweep of white paint, almost pointing to the agonised words.

Judge Smith spoke in his dry way. He knew what she was up to, and he'd seen it all before. 'Miss Mather – I think we have all taken your point. Now, if you could remain in the body of the court . . . ?'

Miss Mather smiled, a dark, secret, winning smile, and moved back front and centre. 'CI5. Criminal Intelligence – a secret organisation, a dangerously omnipotent organisation, answerable, it seems, to no one but its own controller and – '

The Minister rose. 'Mr President, I must protest. We are not here to inquire into CI5 – '

Mather cut in, sharply: 'Aren't we?'

The Minister went on doggedly. 'The object of this inquiry is into the death of Paul Martin Coogan.'

Her point made for her and anxious to drive it fully home, Mather whipped out: 'Very well, I concede. We will confine ourselves to the murder of Paul Coogan – '

The Minister reared up on to his feet, just as he had been about to sit down, lulled by Mather's first words. 'Mr President!'

Judge Smith spoke severely. 'Yes, yes, I agree. Miss Mather, I know you to be a highly skilled counsel. But these cheap tactics do not reflect well, especially when they appear to be aimed at the press.' He moved his hand briefly, left and right. 'When here is where this case will be judged.'

She knew her words had sunk in and done the damage. That one word 'murder' always made people sit up. To allow even more time she bent down to the table to pick up a paper, and whispered to Merlin: 'That's what he thinks!' Then she straightened up and spoke in her firm clear voice. 'The death of Paul Martin Coogan, while held in the custody of CI5. You have seen the official photographs.' She showed the papers and photographs she had picked up from the table. 'And the autopsy report. Paul Coogan died as the result of one, or several, blows that ruptured his spleen. The blow or blows delivered by a clenched fist.'

Cowley was well aware whose fist that was; but, also, he was aware of the circumstances. That was what he had to make these blockheads see – these extraordinarily clever and dedicated blockheads. He was called to the witness stand – the isolated chair – and Miss Mather indicated very clearly the contempt and loathing she felt for him.

'Mr Cowley – you admit that you launched what amounted to a full scale attack on Mr Coogan's house?'

'I ordered a squad operation, yes.'

Mather checked the figures. 'Fourteen men?'

'Fifteen, including myself.' Cowley spoke toughly.

Mather persisted in her line of inquiry. 'Most of them armed?'

'All of them were armed.'

'So,' said Mather, and her head went up and the glint of very white teeth showed for a tantalising instant. 'My full scale attack sounds more accurate than your squad operation.' Scoring that point, she went on quickly before Cowley could reply, flicking out photographs as she spoke. 'You rammed a car in the driveway. You broke down the front door. And then you and your men proceeded to rampage through his house –'

'We searched it!' broke in Cowley.

'Searched it! Carpets ripped up, furniture torn apart.' Photo after photo was whipped up showing the damage. 'Wallpaper stripped away . . .'

'We were looking for something small . . . Drugs . . .'

'Something small?' Mather's contempt lashed across the court. '*Ten pounds* of heroin?'

'They could have split it up. Concealed it in a dozen places – '

'But they hadn't, had they, Mr Cowley? The fact is – you found absolutely nothing!'

'No.'

At Cowley's low and agonised monosyllable, Mather rapped out mercilessly: 'Speak up please, Mr Cowley.'

'No!' Cowley burst out. 'No, we found nothing!'

'Carpets, furniture – all in all damage estimated at several thousand pounds.' She waved the photos. She had Cowley on the hook now, and she drove the barbs in viciously. 'For nothing. And, Mr Cowley, *without a search warrant*!'

'I don't need a warrant – '

'Oh, I see.' The coolness after her savage attack slashed in its own chilling condemnation. 'You don't need a warrant. *You* are outside the laws of this country – '

' – it's within my brief – '

' – you have licence to pillage and assault – and kill?'

Cowley forced himself to hang on to his rapidly vanishing calmness. He stared up from the chair, his forehead a shunter's nightmare of corrugated lines. 'Desperate men call for desperate measures – '

'Desperate men!' Miss Mather's voice flayed him. 'Desperate men?' She swung away from the head-on confrontation with Cowley and faced the reporters, picking up a new set of papers from the cluttered table. She read in a low, even voice, condensing: 'Paul Martin Coogan. Two convictions for drunkenness. One for dangerous driving. John Peter Coogan. One arrest for causing an affray. *No conviction*. These are your desperate men, Mr Cowley.'

With the feeling of the solid earth breaking away from under his feet, Cowley pressed on. 'They're clever. Keep their noses clean. Get others to do their dirty work.'

'In the case of Paul Coogan you should be speaking in the past tense. He wasn't quite so clever, was he? To end up dead in this room – the result of a beating –'

Cowley fairly hurled it out. 'It was just one punch!'

The smile which crossed the lovely and cold face of Miss Mather told Cowley he had just dropped another one. But the questions, the slants, infuriated him, and he must not lose his temper. 'I see,' said Miss Mather in her razor-strop voice. 'So you admit the assault? You admit Paul Coogan *was* punched?'

George Cowley took a single breath. 'In self-defence.'

'Yes, Mr Cowley. We have all of us heard *that* excuse before.' She moved away from the witness chair, a smooth, sinuous motion of great charm. 'No more questions at this time.'

Cowley bore on. 'He attacked my men and –'

'No more questions!'

'You fling out accusations,' said Cowley, beginning to feel his warmth overreaching his cool. His devoted work in building CI5 was at stake and a miserable parcel of half-truths made the department look like a bunch of murdering thugs. 'And then –'

Judge Smith interrupted, quietly but firmly. 'Mr Cowley. You will have your opportunity of putting your side later.'

Miss Mather let the small smile of satisfaction on her face linger just long enough for Merlin to see, then she said in her brisk legal-eagle fashion: 'I would like to call my first witness.'

When the preliminaries had been gone through and John Coogan sat stiffly in the chair, leaning a little to one side, appearing in his bulk and physique to overflow the fragile wooden seat, he responded spendidly to Miss Mather's pointed questions.

'Yes, they held me in a room along the corridor, handcuffed, the whole time. Tight, too. My wrists swelled up for a while after –'

'How many men were in the room with you?' Mather ignored Cowley's infuriated bristle at John Coogan's words.

'Three.'

'Three against one. Why? Did you resist in any way?'

'All I did was keep asking for my lawyer.'

'Which they denied you?'

'Yes.'

Mather half-turned again, so that the reporters got the full benefit of her intense dark eyes. 'They denied you the fundamental and *legal right* of every citizen.'

Cowley was on his feet again. 'We'd made no charge against him.'

Coldly, cuttingly, well aware of the basic nature of the ethics they discussed, and as well aware of the tremendous value the point gave her case, she said: 'Which in my view makes it even more despicable. Mr Coogan – did *they* offer violence to *you*?'

John did not actually swell his chest; but his movement and the way he sat a little straighter gave the impression of a man bulging his chest and biceps. 'They tried . . .'

'He's lying,' snapped Cowley. 'There was no –'

John broke across. 'The three of them. A chair got broke during the scuffle. But,' and he sneered openly at Cowley, 'even with the three of them they couldn't hurt *me*.'

'Because,' suggested Mather, 'you are a powerful man, Mr Coogan. But your brother Paul lacked your physique . . .'

'Paul.' John's face darkened. 'He was just a kid.'

Bodie smothered an enormous yawn, stuck his hands up at the back of his head, tilted his chair back and tried to think of more pleasant surroundings than this sleazy hole and more enticing prospects than his old oppo Ray Doyle up on this rotten deal.

Doyle, his fist held clamped in the spread fingers of his left hand, his head down so that the lights glinted off his curly hair, saw Benny appear at the end of the corridor and gesture.

Frank Williams sat opposite, glowering. Doyle nudged Bodie, almost tipped off the tilted chair, and they went down to speak to Benny out of earshot of Williams. They'd spent a great deal of last evening and night chasing around

London for Parker and had drawn a blank. The club he frequented – Buddy's – was for members only; but that didn't stop Bodie and Doyle. Parker hadn't been seen around. They'd checked out Lorna, a frowsy blonde who was often kind to Henry Parker. She'd known nothing, and her latest, a large and very ugly plug-ugly, had threatened to give the partners a thick ear apiece if they didn't shove off. Mindful of their business, they'd shoved. Mimi, who allowed large areas of her naked skin to come into intimate contact with Hector, her pet snake, had not been helpful either. They'd tooled around the streets, seeing the shop window lights long and streaked in the wet pavements, and they'd turned up a big fat zero. Now Benny, a relatively new addition to CI5, gave them the lead they needed.

'Where?' demanded Doyle.

'Some rooming house in Battersea. Want me to send someone along and bring him in?'

Bodie shook his head. 'Someone he doesn't know? He'd run a mile, go undercover again and we'll never find him.'

'Bodie's right. Just keep an eye on the place. We'll pick him up later.'

Benny nodded at Doyle's words. 'Right.'

Benny cleared off and the partners turned back to their abominable hard wooden seats. John came out of the court room, smiling, cocky, telling Frank Williams he was next. He swung a playful blow at Frank's midriff. 'Keep your guard up, Frank. And box clever.'

Frank smiled and returned the blow. John and Frank indulged in this little harmless bit of sparring as though it was a common occurrence. As Frank went in past Carter ready to take his seat as a witness, Bodie, watching intently, frowned.

Frank gave the court a vivid account of the raid. They'd acted like wild beasts, he said, and one of them had hit him. He touched his face which still bore traces of bruising.

'Why?' demanded Miss Mather.

'I don't know – just hit me, that's all.'

Cowley said in a hard but measured voice: 'Mr Williams. Isn't it a fact you were armed yourself?' As Frank hesitated, Cowley bore on: 'Weren't you carrying a shotgun? Well?'

At last: 'Yes, sir.'

'Mr Williams,' cut in Mather, very quickly. 'Why were you carrying the shotgun?'

Frank knew the answer to this one. That was what David Merlin got paid for. 'There'd been a fox about. Mr Coogan told me to try and get it.'

Mather's voice indicated clearly her triumph. 'You have a legal certificate to own a shotgun?' Frank's yes was obvious. 'And you were within the boundaries of Mr Coogan's private property? Or what should have been his private property. But Cowley and CI5 do not, it seems, respect a man's personal privacy.' Now she hammered directly at Cowley. 'I think that covers the point you raised – except for one thing. Williams here was carrying a shotgun when he was struck down by your man?'

'Yes.'

'Struck down in self defence, no doubt?'

'Of course.'

'Another possible desperate man, as you call them?'

Cowley nodded. 'Yes.'

Mather smiled. Cowley knew he dropped another one. He'd walked into another trap spun by this formidable woman barrister. 'Why then did you not arrest Mr Williams? Why didn't your men bring him in for – questioning?'

'We,' said Cowley, well aware of the water closing over his head, 'were after the Coogans.'

'You were *after* them? As a huntsman stalks game? *After them* with a sense of purpose perhaps – after them with a *vengeance*?'

'No,' Cowley shook his head. 'You don't understand!'

Mather broke across that mercilessly. 'Well, you certainly got one of them, didn't you? You got Paul Coogan!'

With a professional patience on which he no longer prided himself because it was now a part of his professional competence, Judge Smith told Miss Mather: 'Miss Mather

– it *is* just the facts we want.'

'No further questions.'

'Mr Cowley?' Judge Smith half-lifted his eyebrows. 'You wish to cross-examine?'

For a moment Cowley hesitated. But he saw the way the wind was blowing, the way the waves were billowing over his head, and so he decided. 'No. No questions.'

The Minister leaned in, concerned, his face grave. 'George, surely . . . ?'

Cowley whispered fiercely. 'No point. He'll lie through his teeth. Only cloud the issue more.'

'In that case,' said Judge Smith with a relief he kept out of his face and voice. 'I think this would be a convenient time to adjourn for the day.'

Bodie and Doyle took off – fast.

The black Jaguar screeched around the corners and sprayed mud across the pavements. They slid into a sliding halt a ways off from where Benny was keeping the observation on the rooming house in Battersea. One look at Benny's hapless face as he rose from the row of dustbins and walked across to them told them the bad news.

'You let him see you?'

'Sorry, Ray – '

Bodie held in the screaming impatience. 'Where'd he go?'

'Soon as I knew he'd made me I moved in. But there's a back way. I'm sorry.'

'You're sorry!' Bodie looked around at the tenement blocks, the grimy bricks, the air of desolation. A stray cat yowled and streaked across the wet concrete, a wiry spring of fur. Somewhere a dog barked. If he kept that up the place for him was right down here in Battersea. Bodie looked at Doyle. 'What now?'

'Cruise around his old haunts.' Doyle made it firm.

They went back to the car. Benny watched them go. His shoulders slumped. 'I'm sorry,' he said to their backs.

In the car they cruised out and both of them knew this

was a fruitless repetition; but it was something that had to be done.

'You were there,' said Bodie, after a lengthy pause in which his brains had been recycling information. 'Today, in the corridor outside the courtroom when John took a swing at Frank. D'you remember when we first brought Coogan in, how flash he was? Patting his belly, hard as rock – "My brother works out on it sometimes." Didn't he say something like that?' At Doyle's puzzled nod, Bodie went on: 'I was there when you hit Paul Coogan. It was a good punch, economic. But it wasn't going to split doors – or rupture any spleens, either –'

'Bodie – the autopsy report –'

'Said a punch, yes. But why *your* punch?'

The car moved smoothly north from Battersea Park Road towards the bridge. The rain looked to be lifting. The old town would be jumping tonight – as it jumped every night. Doyle looked back from the glistening street. The sun was trying to shine through and already the pavements were drying off.

'John Coogan – ?'

Bodie nodded. '*Big* John. Ex-heavyweight. I can see him – "Come on. Paul – Pauly – hit me hard as you like." And then Paul, trying to live up to his big brother – "Come on, hit me back." '

'And John does –'

'Just like with Frank today. A playful punch at the belly.'

'But John's a pro . . .'

'Even pulling his punches he could still do hell of a lot damage.'

The line of argument was tempting, Doyle saw that, and he considered as the car ran smoothly on and the clouds cleared away and the sun really did begin to shine, ready to create a golden and magical late afternoon and evening. 'No. Thanks, Bodie; but no.'

'Why not?' Bodie kept the fizzing impatience down.

'Paul Coogan showed no signs of pain when we brought him in.'

'Would he? Would he admit to anyone that his brother had hurt him? That'd be weakness in his book.' Bodie saw the way Doyle shifted about, hesitating to speak – hesitating to believe what Bodie now saw as being the true answer. He'd seen Doyle's punch, remember. 'It's possible. You've got to admit it's possible?'

'Maybe. But how would we ever find out?'

'I dunno.' Then Bodie turned the Jaguar up the next left-hand corner, away from the West End. 'Coogan's got a girl at the house.'

The car seemed to know its own way to John Coogan's secluded and luxurious mansion. But this time there was no headlong bashing through doors, no raid, no strife. They parked the car off the verge at the side of the road and then walked carefully along outside the wall under the trees. The sun cast down dappled shadows, and every now and then Bodie or Doyle would chin up to the wall and look over. They knew what they were looking for. The silence was golden and peaceful – and very expensive.

The late warming sun had brought Jill out of the house where she had been cooped up all day. She was nubile, as John demanded. She wore a colourful track suit and she jogged along, mindful of good advice and her figure, of which she was proud. When she heard the disembodied voice float down she stopped and looked around.

'Physical fitness is a cult around here,' said the voice.

Jill looked up. She had a broad, fair face, with wide lips, and now those lips curved into a smile as she saw the tough and remarkably handsome man perched on the brick wall.

'Hi,' said Jill. John might not know; but Jill smiled at all men.

'Hi,' said another voice, and another man appeared on the wall, just as tough, with a round, curly-haired appearance that charmed the impressionable Jill.

Then, at a thought, she frowned. 'I don't think you should be up there.'

'I know. We're fans. Boxing fans. We were hoping to get a glimpse of John Coogan.' The partners took it in turns.

'He hasn't boxed in years.'

'But when he did! He's our hero. Still keeps fit, doesn't he?'

'Oh, yes. Works out every morning.' Here Jill punched a few shadows, fully conscious of the way her figure showed to advantage. Gorgeous, yes, our Jill; but a little dim.

'That's what we heard. Him and his brother Paul.'

Jill felt sad. 'Poor Pauly.'

'Yeah, that was tough. But they did work out together?'

'Sometimes – '

'Trading punches,' said Bodie, pushing a little more. 'That kind of thing ... ?'

'Yes,' Jill said, wide-eyed. 'He hurt him once.'

With a suddenness he had to check as he spoke, Doyle said: 'John hurt Paul?'

'No, no. Paul hurt John.' The two faces on the wall showed disappointment. Jill spoke on, stretching her arms out to expand her chest. 'It was just the other day in fact. Last time they ever sparred together. Paul really hurt Big John.' She smiled. 'His pride as much as anything. Mind you, John hurt him back – '

'What?'

Both men felt they were getting to it when a ferocious voice battered in. 'Jill!'

John Coogan, clad in a track suit as colourful as the one enveloping the delectable form of Jill, came sprinting over the grass towards them. Time to go, decided the CI5 men, regretfully.

'Nice talking with you,' said Bodie.

They dropped down off the wall into the trees. John's face as he bore down on the hapless Jill was extraordinarily ugly.

Cowley passed on the rocket, pronto.

'You fools!' His face showed his wrath. 'You damned fools!' He stormed along with Bodie and Doyle towards the warehouse complex on the morning of the second day of the inquiry. 'To go there – that that house – now!'

'It was a hunch,' said Bodie, doggedly. 'And I think it paid off.'

'D'you know what that Mather woman will make of it?'

'The girl said they sparred together,' Bodie persisted. 'It could let Doyle off the hook. He needs off the hook.'

'Don't you think Coogan is aware of that?'

Doyle said: 'Can't we subpoena the girl and – '

Cowley was scathing. 'What girl? She was on a flight to Spain one hour after you spoke to her. Anything she may have said to you is just – just hearsay – and inadmissable.'

The partners looked glum. It had been so damned promising, too. Finally Bodie got it out. 'I'm sorry, sir. We were just trying to – '

'I know what you were trying to do. And I'm grateful. But the fact of the matter is that it hasn't helped. Not one bit.'

Doyle took a breath. What that girl Jill had said had given him a straw to clutch, and for his own peace of mind he intended to clutch it – tight, damned tight.

'It has me, sir.' He spoke in a forthright way. 'There's a chance – a doubt. Perhaps I didn't kill Paul Coogan.'

Cowley looked at them, seeing them with a clarity he knew they'd never understand. They were a team, and he was their chief, and together they did work that had to be done, distasteful though it was . . . He moved on, jerkily, suddenly hating a great many things, and knowing he didn't understand them all himself.

'See you in court,' said George Cowley, and he spoke wearily. It started raining again.

Chapter Eleven

David Merlin made a deal of capital out of the incident, as Cowley had known he would, and he gave an undertaking to the board that a similar occurrence would not happen again. Then it was Ray Doyle's turn to enter the court room and sit in the witness chair.

True to form Geraldine Mather wore different clothes today, very smart, elegant – and expensive. She was fully conscious of her position as queen bee here, and yet, as Cowley understood with a deadening sensation of futility, the woman was absolutely convinced of her own superior morality, her sense of justice, and as implacably opposed to what she saw as his vile and despotic habits. If she had been like Merlin, now, and not so sincere . . . But she wasn't. She faced Doyle and got to work cutting him down to size.

'Quite an impressive record, Doyle. While with the police you became boxing champion at your weight, a class A marksman with both rifle and handgun.' She tapped the documents which she used as a flail, belting facts of Doyle's record around his head as though they were indictments. 'You are also interested in karate and kendo, sufficiently interested actually to have started a sports club dedicated to those skills – '

Doyle relaxed a bit, which was foolish. 'Yes. It was really for the black kids in my area. They – '

'Obviously,' Mather broke in. 'You are obsessed with violent activities.'

'No – '

'Shooting, boxing, karate . . . ?'

'I,' said Ray Doyle, shifting uneasily on the chair now, 'do other things. I paint –'

'We know that.' Mather put Doyle's artistic pretensions down with the kerbside artists. 'We are here to inquire into one of those other things you do – like brutalising helpless prisoners.'

Cowley rose. 'I must protest –'

Judge Smith leaned down. 'I must, too. *Miss Mather.*'

Miss Mather was off on a new tack. 'Mr Doyle. Isn't it part of your CI5 training to fight with your bare hands?'

'Yes, but –'

'Aren't you taught to break a bone with a single blow? Disembowel at a stroke? Tear a man's gullet? Aren't you taught pressure points, places to hit, to disable, to maim, to kill?'

Again Cowley interjected. 'A normal self-defence course, such as any Commando, any infantryman, would be taught.'

Mather scored the point she knew she'd score. 'Commandos and infantrymen are prepared for *a state of war*. I was not aware that a state of war existed in Britain.' She swung her attack back to Doyle. 'It was you who struck Paul Coogan?'

'He came at me –'

'You struck him? You punched him?'

'Yes, but –'

Mather gave him no chance. 'Struck him so hard that you ruptured his spleen. You killed Paul Coogan, didn't you?'

Almost but not quite truculently, more musingly, Doyle answered. 'I don't know.'

Miss Mather had not expected that particular reply. For a moment her poise faltered, then she bore in again, her verbal attack a vicious swinging drive. 'Come now! We have the evidence that you –'

Doyle interrupted. He blurted his words out. 'I hit him, yes. One punch. But, whether *I* killed him or not . . . ? He played sparring games with his brother. Maybe *he* hit him, maybe –'

Mather didn't like the sound of this and she did not miss the startled and annoyed reaction from David Merlin. She bit out her words sharply. 'No more questions.'

But Doyle was wound up. 'D'you think I *want* to think I killed him? Life's important – any life, and – '

With a vicious snap, a pettish crack of sound, Mather ripped out: *'No more questions.'*

Doyle stopped. He looked around the court, a little dazed. If they wanted the truth it was only a legal business for them. But he was the man in the middle. It was his conscience and his agonised thoughts he would have to live with. For Raymond Doyle this whole nasty business was no clever legal game.

Sitting waiting his turn, Bodie could guess with shrewd accuracy at the torment Ray Doyle was going through in there. Doyle was conscientious where Bodie was inclined to a raffishness in matters of pettifogging detail. Bodie did not think Doyle had put enough power into that single punch to rupture a man's spleen. But if that man had been knocked about, earlier on, by a big rough, tough ex-boxer like John Coogan? John had been hurt by Paul, no doubt of that, as the absent Jill had explained. Perhaps, this time, the big fellah forgot to pull his punches?

David Merlin sidled out of the court, gestured to John who rose. The two walked along the corridor immersed in deep conversation. Bodie glared hotly after them and heard John exclaim: 'No! I couldn't have!' Then they passed out of earshot.

John lowered his head, like an angry bull. 'Me, kill Pauly? My own brother?'

Merlin spoke quietly. 'Is it possible?'

John Coogan's big hands curled into fists. Those fists were hard, knobbly, massive with crushing power.

Merlin persisted. 'You did spar with him?'

'Sometimes. But just in fun.'

'No.'

John looked surprised, letting his hands unclench, looking down on Merlin. Merlin looked annoyed, determined.

'No. *You never sparred with him.* You never played games with him. You never laid a hand on him. Understand?'

The two stood for a moment, then John nodded, dumbly, and Merlin walked off, stiffly, back into the court room. A moment later Doyle emerged. He ran a hand through his curly hair. He looked absolutely fed-up. He slumped down beside Bodie in the chair tipped against the corridor wall.

'How did it go?'

Doyle made a grimace. 'Lousy. She made a monkey of me.'

'Well – you did give her a head start.'

'She's a dragon.'

'She's a woman.' Bodie half-closed his eyes. 'And a damned good-looking one.'

'Well, it'll be your turn soon.'

Bodie smiled. 'Don't worry. I'm not monkey material.' Carter leaned out from the door and beckoned. Confidently, Bodie climbed to his feet. He shook his shoulders. 'A woman. And I never yet met a woman I couldn't handle. I'll just fix her with my famous smile . . .'

Sitting in the witness chair after the necessary preliminaries Bodie put that famous smile on his face and waited for the onslaught.

Mather said: 'William, Andrew, Phillip Bodie?'

These were the names he had been blessed with; but he would only answer to Bodie.

'Yes,' he said brightly. 'All princes. I was such a *regal* looking baby.'

Mather consulted her indispensable documents. The charm she could feel exuding from this witness had to be used . . . 'You left school at fourteen?'

'There was nothing more they could teach me.'

As Mather was also considering that cockiness would also have to be used, Judge Smith spoke up. 'Just answer the questions, Mr Bodie.'

'You joined the Merchant Navy? And you jumped ship three years later at Dakar?'

'Yes. Had an altercation with the skipper. There was this girl, you see. His girl. Took a shine to me, and – '

Now was the time to use the charm and the pathetic arrogance where it would put this man where he belonged. He needed, as he would phrase it, to be taken down a peg or two. She was fully conscious of her own femininity, and she was also aware that this man Bodie was conscious of her as a woman. This, she would rectify at once, and cut him down, cut him down ruthlessly.

'Your machismo is of no interest to us, Mr Bodie. Merely your background. Your violent background. Bouncer in an African club. Gun running for both sides during the Congo wars. Mercenary soldier in Angola. Biafra. Some dubious activities in Jordan. And then back here to join the Army, where you became a sergeant with the Paras. Then seconded to the SAS. And CI5. It appears you hire out your – body – for *any* nefarious activity so long as the price is right.'

Cowley stormed up. 'Mr President !'

'I'll rephrase that,' carried on Miss Mather with smooth competence. 'You hire out your – experience – is that right, Mr Bodie ?'

'That'll do,' said Mr Bodie.

'And your greatest talent is dealing out death, violence, mayhem ? How many men have you killed, Mr Bodie ?'

'I don't remember.'

'You don't remember !' Making the most of this, Miss Mather faced the court and although she did not lift her hands and arms, as though beseeching heaven, the appearance she gave was of a great and sorrowful – and condemnatory – appeal. 'Do you hear that ? This is a man who is a member of CI5 – '

Bodie's cool had evaporated. 'You toss a grenade into the brush and who knows how many you get ? The jungle – it's – '

'The jungle !' Miss Mather broke across, triumphantly. 'Yes, Mr Bodie. I think that is where you belong !'

Bodie digested that. He didn't much care for the implications this beautiful but bitchy woman was tossing his way. His famous smile had disappeared. Somehow she made what he had done sound dirty. Hell – didn't she know life was a jungle, a nasty horrible smelly jungle, all the time? She must have seen something of the seamy side of life in her work as a barrister. She couldn't be living up an ivory tower, could she?

Now Miss Mather bore in again. She spoke with that sudden and expert shifting from emphasis to cool examination.

'You were part of the squad that attacked Mr Coogan's house? You were the man who struck down Frank Williams?'

'Yes, he had a gun, and –'

'And you had a gun, too – and were ready to use it.'

Bodie's cool had been evaporating ever more swiftly. Jungles or no, this clever bitch was getting under his skin. His anger burst out at her latest suggestion. 'Look, the informer told us there was heroin. People kill for heroin –'

'Informer?'

Bodie collapsed back in the seat, horrified by this latest example of the disasters his temper could lead him into. Cowley and the Minister glanced swiftly at each other as Miss Mather turned sharply to stare at Cowley.

'Is that correct? You set up this whole disgusting affair on the word of a common informer?'

'It frequently,' said Cowley, stiffly, cautiously, 'brings results.'

Miss Mather looked down her nose at him. 'I want him here. I want to question this informer. I want to see how he measures up against the respectable image of John Coogan.' She stared directly at Cowley, dominatingly. 'His name, Mr Cowley?'

Cowley saw the way Bodie had winced back the moment the words had left his lips; but Cowley was confident that common sense would prevail. After all, the most ignorant of criminal procedures knew you just didn't go bandying the names of paid informers around in the open. But Mather was pressing and the judge was waiting. Cowley glanced at the Minister and then, slowly, said:

Mr President. This is restricted information.'

Miss Mather bustled on, like a ferret on the scent of a rabbit. 'Mr President. I insist.' She saw Judge Smith hesitating, not looking at all happy. 'Of course, if you wish to be party to a cover up . . . ?'

Judge Smith said: 'One moment.'

Cowley watched as the judge conferred with his fellow board members, Stennard and McKay. He stood squarely, head up, feeling the solid earth sliding away from under him. 'To name him in open court . . . It could put him at grave risk . . . It would be irresponsible!'

The court finished its conference and Judge Hall said in a gravelly voice: 'Nevertheless, Mr Cowley – '

Harold McKay, his dislike of all the doings of CI5 open and evident, cut in forcibly. 'We insist upon it.'

Cowley felt the last of the solid earth go. He was at a complete loss.

McKay felt the reins of power in his hands.

'Cowley – this court is *ordering* you to – '

'Parker,' said Cowley, and the anguish in his voice was unmistakable. 'Henry Parker.' He stared directly at Miss Mather. 'And may God help him!'

John Coogan and Frank Williams, sitting across from him, shared Doyle's interest as Bodie came out. Bodie looked less than charmed with life and himself in particular.

'Well,' said Doyle. 'How did you make out?'

Bodie stared evilly at his partner and those mobile lips thinned out. Bodie did not answer in words. He stuck his top lip out, lifted his arms, bent at the elbows, and flapped his hands under his armpits. Doyle had to smile. The formidable Miss Mather had made a monkey out of Doyle by his own admission; she had served his partner the same way.

The corridor filled with hubbub as the members came out, reporters racing for the phones to spread this titillating titbit of news to the world. CI5 agents moved warily, for that was the way they were trained. David Merlin emerged, smoothing down his hair after shouldering along, found John and Frank and immediately bent down to whisper agitatedly to them.

John's face set into so ugly a pattern he would have scared the devil sent to carry him away. 'Parker!'

At his side Frank banged a fist on to his knee. '*Nosey* Parker.'

The crowd exiting swirled past, and Cowley washed up on its skirts to finish up by Doyle and Bodie. Bodie looked at the floor, then, being Bodie, looked up fair and square. 'I'm sorry, sir. Just blurted it out.'

Doyle said, looking from one to the other: 'Blurted what out?'

'About Parker.'

Doyle understood how a woman like that could get under your skin. Her very self-righteousness was the clincher. She thought she was right, and her colossal ego told her she was right. But she'd got through to Bodie, that was clear, and the thought uncharitably occurred to Doyle that perhaps the fabulous Miss Geraldine Mather didn't belong to the same club. That would explain a great deal; but the fact would still remain. She sincerely believed that what she was doing was right. And, of course, in a civilised society she was right. Indisputably.

As these sombre thoughts crossed Doyle's mind as he stood with the others digesting the unwelcome news he spotted the hulking shoulders of Big John and his massive head going past over the crush towards the door. As the crowd thinned, no doubt helped to spread out by those bulky shoulders and an elbow or three, Doyle saw Frank Williams hurrying along towards the exit. Both men moved with a determination that told they were in a hurry.

He pointed them out and Cowley, grim-faced, told them: 'Stay close. But stay clear, too! Don't give that – woman – another opportunity of . . .'

But already Bodie and Doyle were hurrying off, skipping past the tail end of the people leaving. Cowley stared after them. The lines on his craggy face were deeply indented. He could feel the tiredness in his bones, dragging at his muscles, twitching his belly. He ached. And that blasted bullet in his leg was playing him up unmercifully...

The tail the partners stuck on John Coogan and Frank Williams turned out to be as perfect a tail as they'd ever done. Where those two went, the partners went, too...

They were led over a large part of the familiar stamping ground of the twilight zone of London and as the light faded and the damned rain mizzled down again they tooled the black Jag up the latest little sleazy side alley and stopped before the latest sleazy little club.

As Bodie said: 'John Coogan is pursuing his enquiries –'

'– and with his contacts he's got a darned sight better chance of finding Parker than we have,' finished Doyle.

'So,' said Bodie. 'We wait. And where *he* goes –'

'– *we* go.'

The sign over the doorway to the club set in a shadowed slot of darkness shone out, its bulbs weak and speckled. 'Buddy's' the sign read. 'Members only.'

This was the club where Parker claimed he was well-liked, where the partners had already made enquiries only to be met by negative shakes of the head and an indifference to their urgency. Inside, the place was as sleazy as the surroundings outside. The lights were dim. Very dim. The tables looked as though they'd gone down with a ship in a gale and only been salvaged along with something else. The walls bore specks and splotches of damp, along with a few crudely-painted representations of quasi-Reubens ladies remarkable only for their contortions. The bottle display was discreet. It possessed the unhappy aptitude of being broken up with great frequency. The tatty place boasted a juke box, which played discs not above a couple of years old. The customers lined the bar or sat at the tables, and their conversations were limited.

When John Coogan shouldered in he brought a breath of toughness, an air of the hurricane. He looked about, a plug-ugly come to demoniac life.

'Out,' said Big John. 'Everybody. Out the back way Move!'

No one was going to argue with Big John, including those few – those very few – who thought he was just an ex-boxer.

Frank helped some of the customers on their way; but most of them were only too thankful to be able to get away without having their ears cropped. The back exit handled them, they crowded in a bunch. John half-turned and surveyed the bar.

'Everybody,' he boomed. 'Except *you*!'

Henry Parker cowered back on his bar stool, feeling the hard wood of the bar against his side, feeling his guts all squishy squashy and sloshing about inside.

Sammy, the big barman with the cropped hair and the anchor tattooed on his forearm, put down his cloth slowly. John nodded to him, quite affably.

'You're closing early, Sammy.'

The barman nodded. He was closing early.

When Sammy had gone and only Parker, cringing, was left with John and Frank, the silence crept in, soft and deadly. The rubicund ladies smiled down, all dimples and curves. The lights in their fly-blown shades shone discreetly. The juke box sat, shiny and chromiumed and dented, silent.

John advanced deliberately on the informer.

He towered. He looked like a grizzly bear about to devour a venturesome trapper caught without his trusty Sharps.

'Grass on me, Parker? On *me*?'

Frank put his hand into his pocket and pulled out a hammer. It was a new hammer, with a forged steel handle, and it gleamed with a menace quite lost on the terrified Parker. Then Frank put his hand into his other pocket. When Parker saw what he pulled out, the informer started to scream. A huge and meaty hand clapped over his mouth.

'Grass on me, Parker? On *me*?'

The rain sifted down and mizzled an orange glow over the dim lighting of Buddy's club. The black Jaguar crouched under the rain tucked into the kerb, and Bodie and Doyle sat hunched, watching, not speaking much, waiting for John Coogan to draw a blank and lead them to more successful haunts to find Parker.

Presently, Bodie said in a way more petulant than he cared for himself: 'That Mather woman. She isn't a woman! She's an automaton. A freak. An approximation of the real thing.'

'Just because she didn't faint at your smile?'

But both of them knew there was more to Geraldine Mather than that. Doyle looked through the rain-smeared window. The sign telling an indifferent world that members only were welcome at Buddy's went out.

A faint noise seeped through the falling rain, an old pop tune belting out on an off-speed jukebox. Both CI5 men sat up.

Doyle shouted: 'Move. Move!'

They were out of the car and running through the rain towards the club. Their shoes made little splitter-spatter sounds and the noise of the jukebox increased.

They hit the door, shoulder to shoulder, and went through in a rending crash of wood and glass. The dimness of the outside was matched by that inside. They belted on, kicking a few tables and chairs out of the way. The jukebox was really turned up, on full gain, pitching out an avalanche of sound.

On a table lay a six-inch nail.

Doyle hauled up and Bodie looked about in the dimness, searching for someone – anyone – and seeing only shadows and the dark fretted outlines of tables and chairs, the empty bar.

A single drop fell on the table.

A single drop of blood.

Holding the six-inch nail in his hand, Doyle looked up.

Bodie looked up as well, up to the wall above the table.

The faces of both agents of CI5 ricked back in horrified grimaces. They looked up, as Doyle held the six-inch nail and the spot of blood stained the table, they looked up at the wall and its blasphemous freight . . .

Chapter Twelve

The third day of the court of inquiry settled down, promising the finish for CI5. Everyone was aware of the electric discharges of power here, the head on collision between civilised behaviour and the law of the jungle. Cowley paced the corridor outside as the court convened, and he kept on looking at the empty chairs where his two star agents should be sitting.

He turned back in his pacing and spoke most uncivilly to Carter, stolid on the door.

'Where are they?'

'Haven't heard a word.'

'Locate them,' ordered Cowley. 'And let's hope they're not recalled to give evidence.'

With that, feeling the tiredness and the damned bullet in his leg, he limped into the court room.

Cowley's two star agents were doing their own pacing – up and down a hospital corridor.

Doyle was doing most of the pacing. Bodie calmly consulted his watch.

'The court,' Bodie reminded Doyle, 'is now in session.'

Before Doyle could make an answer – and what he might have said defied imagination – the door opened and the doctor came out, fiddling with his stethoscope, not looking happy. He was a young man, weighed down with problems; but he braced up as he met the full barrage from Bodie and Doyle.

'Well?' demanded Doyle.

'Out of the question – '

'Can he be moved?'

The doctor left off fiddling with his stethoscope to spread his hands. 'The man's in shock – '

Doyle brushed that aside. 'Doctor – can he be moved?'

The doctor hesitated. Then: 'Look – why can't you just take a statement?'

That was answer enough for Ray Doyle. He started for the door and, with a brief and bleak smile for the doctor, Bodie followed.

The court room temporarily rigged up in the interrogation room that was itself merely an old warehouse room was more packed than ever. Reporters knew that this was going to be the day of decision. Every one of them looked to the come-uppance of CI5 and its chief, George Cowley. Everyone was in place and the floor was Cowley's.

He had formed CI5, created it, motivated it, given it its teeth, its brains and its conscience. The brief handed to him by the Government concerned over the growing incidence of violent crime and by crimes committed with a full arsenal of sophisticated modern equipment had been to beat the villains at their own game. This Cowley had been sincerely attempting to do.

Now he spoke with deep feeling. And he shook Mather.

'I – *we* – have all heard a great deal of argument from Miss Mather. Emotional argument.' As Miss Mather started to protest at this, Cowley went on: 'But, backed in the main, by hard facts.'

Geraldine Mather closed her mouth. She was unsure what was going on; as she sat back in her chair next to Merlin she owned she had not expected this. Cowley was going on.

'Hard facts. Yes, they are hard – and they are facts.' He looked at Mather, and then away. 'That is the tragedy of it.'

He was in his stride now, and Mather wasn't going to protest and object now. 'She has used me as her whipping boy because I founded CI5. But I didn't!'

A rustle greeted this, of surprise and displeasure, but

Cowley swung around to face all those people who stared at him.

'You did. Society did. This society did. If there were no fires, you wouldn't need firemen. And in God's name – and I invoke Him sincerely – I wish you would make my job, my organisation, redundant. I wish you would make the streets clean again. I wish you would give every man, whatever his colour or creed, the right to be – to feel – safe again. But it isn't to be, not yet. And so you need me. Like it or not, you need CI5.'

He did not stop speaking; but he was flaying them with his words, and he knew it, and they knew it.

'You need CI5, which is why I am asking, pleading, with you – don't destroy us. Don't cut us down. Not until you have something better to put in our place. Miss Mather has seized upon the world jungle. Aye, in the popular vernacular *that is where it is at!* A jungle. With mad beasts stalking through it. And we are the hunters.'

Now he turned his attention fully on Geraldine Mather.

'That was your argument, too. Did I set out to hunt Coogan down? The answer is – yes. It will always be yes, so long as there are beasts like Coogan left to hunt.' Miss Mather might have attempted to interrupt the torrent then, but Cowley snatched up a sheaf of papers from his table. 'You displayed photos – carpets ripped up, cars dented – but what about these?'

The photographs were hideous. Young-old people lying helplessly in hospital cots, blood, withdrawal, bruises, twisted bodies – 'Faces grown old before they were ever young. Destroyed and wrecked by drug addiction. Girls, scarcely out of their teens, selling their bodies, their experience, to the highest bidder. Not – ' He bore down on Miss Mather now, speaking to her personally. ' – for the same purpose as Bodie, Miss Mather. Not for the same purpose at all.'

She just sat there, and Cowley went remorselessly on.

'Respectable businessmen – beaten up because they bucked the price of extortion and bully boys. These are the streets *we* have to walk, not the bright ones – *the mean ones!* Devoid of hope and all humanity. We walk them, and we brush aside some of the dirt – not much! – just some of the dirt, so that there is less to offend when *you* come along.'

Small sweat drops beaded like pearls along Cowley's corrugated forehead. He took a deep breath. 'And now you are trying to take away whatever teeth we have left. Why? Why? Because someone got hurt? Because a man died? And I regret that, I didn't want it. A man died – and you want to close down the whole hospital? Because, like it or not, that is what we are – the surgeons. A messy, sometimes bloody job. And, oh, yes, our knives are sharp, and we have to operate fast and quickly, even clumsily on occasion, to excise the disease.'

He had captured the attention of everyone in the court now, captured it utterly – with, perhaps, just two exceptions . . .

'The disease hurts. But so does the surgeon's knife. Which would you prefer? It's your choice.'

So George Cowley sat down to a small but spontaneous burst of applause from the reporters, which, he felt, to be redundant and not in keeping with the high seriousness of what he was attempting to say. This wasn't a show, for God's sake.

The Minister leaned across. 'Well done, George.'

Cowley breathed out, took a breath, said: 'I can do no better.'

And Miss Mather leaned towards David Merlin to say: 'I told you. No fool.'

Slowly, she stood up. She was fully aware of the situation, the expectancy, the murmur that passed around the room. Everyone wanted to know how she would react. She could almost admit, now to a tiny quiver of pity for George Cowley. A man of that calibre ought to have cut out better things for himself in life . . .

She waited for the court to subside to silence – to complete silence. Only when not a sound disturbed the bleak barrenness of the room would she speak.

'Mr Cowley.' She paused. The moment poised on the

threshold of a man's destruction, of the smashing of his beliefs. But Miss Mather's beliefs upheld her. 'It would be untrue – *patently* untrue – if I were to say I was not moved by your final plea. A passionate plea – from the heart – and made even more poignant because – ' And here Miss Mather used her scalpel devastatingly. 'Because *I* believe *you* truly believe in everything you said.'

A surprised murmur – perhaps a reproving murmur – rippled around the court. But Miss Mather had no doubts.

'Misguided though it may be, you believe in your own, twisted argument! Believe in your own *right*, your own omnipotence, and that is the danger we face here.'

She appeared to dismiss Cowley with that. She turned, deliberately, facing the reporters, capturing the attention of the press bench, her words a ringing declamation.

'And the dangers are real, believe me! They have already cost an innocent young man his life, and – '

She was interrupted not by Cowley or the Minister, not even by the judge, making an objection. A disturbance began at the door and Carter, quickly stepping aside, waved on the party entering swiftly. Miss Mather frowned and swivelled to stare.

Doyle and Bodie entered. It was clear from their faces that the time for fun and games had passed, if, ever, there had been such a time. They wasted no time. They pushed the wheelchair before them. Propped in the wheelchair Henry Parker, informer, looked like death.

The pillows propping his thin body were little whiter than his face. He was swaddled in blankets – red blankets. Lying on the red blankets his arms ended not in normal hands, but in two monstrous swathings of bandages, massive rounds obscuring his hands and extending up his wrists. A sheen of perspiration on his face, his long lugubrious face, gave him somehow the look of a desperately sick man. Which he was.

Miss Mather was outraged by this clumsy intrusion just as she was driving the last nail into Cowley's coffin.

She protested vehemently. 'Mr President!'

Ray Doyle shoved the chair down between the seats and

wheeled it up front and centre. He didn't care any more – for the niceties of legal protocol, for this obsessed woman who lived in a make-believe world, or for the gang centred around Coogan – he just shoved the chair with the shattered Parker propped in it like a mummy being carted around the British Museum. He looked up, and his face was set.

'You wanted the informer. Well, you've got him!'

The buzz was tremendous. Reporters craned. Judge Smith looked helplessly at Cowley.

Cowley saw that look, snapped: 'Doyle! Bodie!'

The partners brooked no argument as they wheeled poor old Parker into the front and centre position. They were steamed up and, for their own sakes as well as Cowley's, they felt they had every right to be.

Bodie called across: 'The spirit of the law, sir. *She* demanded Henry Parker. And she's got him!'

From the front and centre where everyone had a good chance to gain a very close look at Parker, the partners wheeled him directly up to Miss Mather. The wheelchair halted, quivering, as she took a hesitant step back. Her eyes were wide. Her colour was gone. Her hand crept up to her throat . . . She didn't know what to make of this, had no immediate answer to handle what was happening.

Doyle said in his cutting way: 'We found him nailed. *Nailed!*' With a gesture of supreme contempt, Doyle tossed the six inch nail on to the table before David Merlin and Miss Mather. The metal clanged with the impact. 'Nailed to a wall, by – person or persons unknown.'

Bodie took over, his voice lifting. '*But*. As his identity was unknown until announced in *this* court – ' He moved his lithe body around, quite deliberately, turning to stare directly and challengingly at Miss Mather, homing in on her ' – we must assume that it was as a direct result.'

He moved in closer. He was eyeball to eyeball with the female barrister, the legal eagle, the formidable Miss Geraldine Mather. He spoke a last few words, and they were strictly for her. 'How does it feel to play Pontius Pilate?'

The two were locked in a statis of bitter anger and of understanding and shocked horror. Miss Mather *saw* . . .

The day was waning, once again, as is the habit of days, and the rain couldn't make up its mind. The rain didn't seem to know whether to drop down or to lash a hurricane. Either way, it rained, and Cowley and his men hauled up their coat collars as they left the warehouse complex that, serving as a temporary CI5 HQ, had for the past three days served as the setting for a court of inquiry that had turned up some interesting under-stones life. Miss Mather would never be quite the same again; but Cowley, for one, fancied she'd grown over the last day, at the least.

'The last minute witness,' he was saying as they moved towards his white Rover 3500.

'Whatever,' said Bodie, warmly. 'It worked.'

'Partially.' As Doyle and Bodie stared a little surprised, he explained what he meant. It was not nice. 'We didn't get Coogan.'

'We will,' said Bodie. 'One day. Anyway, we survived.'

'By the skin of our teeth.' Cowley wouldn't easily forget the sinking sensations of going down with his department. But they had survived. He'd not had to mention anything about eggs and omelettes. But the work that CI5 did was of crucial importance in the fight against crime. That was the brief he had been handed, which he had attempted to honour, and would go on fighting for, believing. In a civilised society the citizenry wouldn't need him, or Bodie or Doyle; but as they did he saw the future as plainly as any man could hope to discern that vague and misty country.

'The inquiry didn't exactly exonerate us with a non-proven verdict.'

'But we did survive,' persisted Bodie.

'To fight another day. Fancy a beer on that?'

'Fine.' Bodie looked pleased, hunching his head in the collar of his coat. 'Doyle?'

Doyle shook his head. 'No, thanks. I'm tired. Think I'll have an early night.'

Doyle walked off. The other two looked after him and Bodie would have followed; but Cowley put a restraining hand on his arm.

'Leave it, Bodie.' The words were crisp.

'Yeah.' Bodie gazed after his partner. Doyle walked slowly, hunched, hands in pockets. The slanting lines of rain formed a curtain between them, a silvery beaded curtain with a ripple of bouncing bubbles at its hem. Doyle looked distant and fragile, walking away like that. Then Bodie brightened. Ray Doyle was Ray Doyle – 'nuff said. 'He'll soon forget it.'

'No.' Cowley, too, stared after Doyle. 'No, never. But he'll learn to come to terms with it.'

Tomorrow – or the day after – the rain would stop and the sun would shine. Cowley was right. It wouldn't be easy – well, what was easy except getting yourself killed? – but no superficial slickness of pseudo-psychology was going to help, either. Ray Doyle would slug this battle out on the inside of his skull, alone. And, Bodie would take bets, he'd win.

'Come on,' said Cowley, heading for his car, flashing his keys out. 'The beer's on me.'

Bodie said: 'Great!'

'And,' Cowley told him. 'The Scotch is on you!'

SEASON OF THE MACHETE

by James Patterson

The bestselling terror-thriller of berserk butchery and cold conspiracy

FEBRUARY 24, 1974 SOMEWHERE IN THE NEVADA DESERT:
The bosses of organised crime and the top dogs of America's secret government plot the spectacular takeover of a romantic resort island. They have approved '*Machete*' – the brainchild of Carrie and Damian Rose, husband and wife team, supreme artists in strike-and-hide assassination.

Their plan:
Create terror, confusion and collapse through the random slaughter of innocent people.

Their price:
Total anonymity and $1,250,000.

APRIL 30, 1975 ON THE ISLAND OF SAN DOMINICA:
A sunbather comes upon a bloody machete in the sand. Nearby, the butchered bodies of a boy and girl.

THE SEASON HAS BEGUN . . .

SEASON OF THE MACHETE is an explosively compelling thriller of shattering violence and horrific political treachery. It will hold the reader in its unrelenting grip from the first massacre to the devastating climax.

0 7221 67261 THRILLER FICTION 95p